CIN'S MARK

BY

ZETTA ELLIOTT

Rosetta
Press

*for
the unburied*

CIN'S MARK

1.

With everything going on in my life right now, I take peace wherever I can find it. And these days, that's in The Woodlands. It sounds like a park or some forest out in the countryside, but it's not. It's a cemetery in West Philly.

Never thought I'd say this, but I like walking with the dead. Not with them, exactly. Around them—and on top of them, I guess. Point is, they're there. Silent. Accepting. The dead make great company.

Three days a week I take Freddie for a walk after school. Since her double hip replacement, Mrs. Whitmore can't make it up the hill anymore so she pays me to bring her yappy little terrier to his happy place. When we're on the street, Freddie barks at just about everything that moves—cars, other dogs, squirrels, fallen leaves blown by the wind. But once we reach the cemetery, even the dog shows respect.

There's just something about this place. Maybe it's because it's so old. The cemetery opened in 1840 but before that it was this rich White dude's home. His name was Hamilton (not *that* Hamilton). He built a mansion and then planted trees and other things to make his home look just like some lord's fancy estate back in England.

I catch bits and pieces of the tours they give while I'm walking Freddie sometimes. That's how I know there are two-hundred-year-old trees in this cemetery that never would have grown on this side of the Atlantic if they hadn't been brought over here by Hamilton. Imagine that—being so rich you can make the world look just the way you want. Hamilton's been dead a long time. He might not be too happy about his mansion sitting in the middle of a cemetery, but he definitely put his stamp on this corner of the city.

I think about death a lot. Not 'cause I'm tired of living. It's just that some days it feels like death is all around me. And I'm not talking about drive-bys or cops gone wild. Mr. Jackson passed a couple of weeks ago. He was our next-door neighbor and a really cool guy. Then he had a stroke and his daughter came up from Florida. She said she was going to take him back down south but Mr. Jackson had another stroke and died before that could happen. Maybe he died on purpose. Mr. Jackson didn't really like hot weather. Both of us prefer fall when the temperature drops and the leaves turn red and gold. We always invited Mr. Jackson over to our place for Thanksgiving dinner. He liked pumpkin pie. My favorite is sweet potato so Mama would bake both.

Sometimes when I'm walking Freddie I imagine Mr. Jackson's there beside me. I could talk about anything with him. I think being so old made him easy to trust. Plus Mr. Jackson had seen it all. He got drafted and sent to Viet Nam when he was just eighteen. He lost friends over there and then came back to Philly and lost more friends to heroin. Mr. Jackson never sugarcoated stuff. He told me about having PTSD and how much he regretted walking out on his wife and kids. He might not have been the best husband or father, but Mr. Jackson was a really good friend. I miss him.

One thing we used to talk about was my Uncle Kev. He always seemed more like a big brother than an uncle since he was Mama's baby brother. He died almost two years ago and Mama took it real hard. We're both hurting but I guess it shows in different ways.

I keep my feelings inside most of the time. Mama looks after everybody but herself. She just does and does and does until she can't do no more. Then she crawls under the covers and sleeps for days. When she's in bed, Mama sleeps like the dead. She forgets about all her problems—and me, too.

I can take care of myself. Picking up odd jobs around the neighborhood gives me a little pocket change, which means I don't have to bother Mama when I need my hair cut or there's no food in the house. I keep my grades up and I keep my head down outside of school. I make sure the apartment is always neat and tidy in case Ms. Donovan stops by. She's our caseworker. I know she's got a job to do but we were doing just fine till some nosy neighbor reported Mama for neglect. Now it's up to me to make our lives look as normal as possible. Otherwise I could get put into foster care and I don't know what would happen to Mama. I know she needs help but so did Kev and the government sure didn't take care of him. He was innocent but they locked him up anyway.

Kev's homeboy Juan got one of his boys to paint a mural at the corner of our block. Mama and I went to the unveiling and lit a candle for Kev, but truth is, most days I go around the block just to avoid seeing my uncle's smiling face on that wall. We say "RIP" all the time when someone gets taken out too soon, but I don't know if everybody rests in peace. After Kev's death some activists held a rally in front of the courthouse. I wasn't there but I watched it on the news. Folks were shouting, "No justice, no peace!" Well, there was no justice for Kev. So how can I believe he's resting in peace?

Mama once said that Kev's death might make things better. I'm not so sure about that. And Mama? These days I don't know if she believes things *can* get better. There's a group here in Philly that raises money to bail poor folks out of jail. That's good. It'll help a whole bunch of other families, but it won't help ours.

At least having Kev here at The Woodlands means he's close enough to visit. Not that Mama has been by lately. She hardly ever leaves the house these days. When Kev died, we didn't have enough money to give him a big funeral. That's not what he wanted, anyway—he said so in the letter he left behind. But some folks thought that meant we didn't care about him or were ashamed of how he died, which isn't true.

Nobody said anything to our face, but I heard some folks muttering about what a shame it was that Mama chose to "burn up her kin." When I die, I definitely want to be cremated but I want my ashes scattered instead of buried. Maybe someplace peaceful like The Woodlands or way out in the ocean. Why pay all that money to let someone drain your blood? Just so you can look like rubber and lie underground in a fancy box that costs as much as a small car? No, thanks.

We did the best we could for Kev. My friend's aunt took up a collection at her church and on our block. I know it's not right, but sometimes I wonder where those folks were when Kev needed bail money. Still, their generosity got us a tiny plot here at The Woodlands. There's no headstone, just a small bronze plaque set in the ground.

You have to know exactly where you're going to find Kev's grave. It's not like the big monuments some rich folks put up back in the day—elegant angels and pointy obelisks with the family name carved into the stone. Some of them even curbed their plots. Imagine wrapping a granite wall around your family's headstones and adding steps to make visitors feel like they're entering a private room—even though they're outdoors! Then there are the cradle graves, which look like someone put a stone bathtub on top of whoever died. But instead of water, the tubs are filled with soil. The cemetery even has a team of special gardeners to keep those flowerbeds looking nice.

We don't have anything like that for Kev, but I always stop by during my walks with Freddie. I was six when Kev got locked up and almost ten when they finally let him out. The charges were dropped but he never got an apology. After Kev took his own life, Mama talked about suing the city. She even met with a couple of lawyers. They told her it would take years for the lawsuit to get before a judge, but they had no answer when Mama asked how to put a price on her baby brother's life.

When Kev got out of jail, he came to live with us but the person we knew before was gone. In his place was a ghost who never smiled and flinched if you tried to touch him. Mama said to give him time to heal, but Kev needed more than time. We didn't know how to help him and so he did the only thing he could think of to help himself. At least that's how I like to think about it. Kev wasn't trying to hurt anybody—not us, not himself. He was hurting already and just needed a way to make the pain stop.

Mr. Jackson once told me that suicide was an act of courage: "Most folks think it's a coward's way out, but they're wrong—dead wrong." He said lots of veterans take their own lives and soldiers sure aren't cowards. "Sometimes a man's just seen too much," Mr. Jackson explained. "Life plays like a movie behind your eyes and you do what you gotta do to make it stop."

I'm only thirteen but I've seen a lot already. Like Kev, Mama needs help. I hope if it ever gets to be too much, I'll be brave enough to find us a way out.

2.

Every school's got mean girls. At my school, we've got hyenas—a pack of pretty, petty, sometimes vicious eighth-grade girls who turn on one another as soon as somebody bigger and stronger shows up. Keysha, Raquel, and Amina were howling with laughter just a minute ago. Now their heads are tucked down and they've left Janae to fend for herself.

Janae and I were friends before she joined the pack last year. Now I guess she's too cool to be seen with me. But I still feel bad for Janae because Aunt Jackie's on a mission. I doubt she got called in because the principal's nowhere to be seen. That means Aunt Jackie heard something about Janae from the talking heads at her salon. She must have gotten one of the cafeteria ladies to let her in the side door.

Aunt Jackie's no joke. All the kids on our block call her that and she treats all of us like we're family. I think I remember meeting Janae's mom back in the day, but for the past five years, Aunt Jackie's been raising Janae and her twin brothers. And as my mama would say, "Jackie don't take no mess."

"Why do you keep looking at them? Your little friends can't help you now. Matter of fact, I bet they the ones got you acting like this," she says. "Did they put you up to it? Huh? 'Cause I know I didn't raise no bully. Maybe I ought to go over there and have a word with them, too. Is that what you want—to share the blame?"

"No!" Janae cries, desperately clutching her aunt's wrist. Like that could stop Aunt Jackie once she's made up her mind.

"No what?"

Janae drops her aunt's wrist and stares at the floor. "No, ma'am."

"Then you better fix your face and go handle your business. I ain't got all day to be standing here waiting on you. I got customers waiting on *me*. Well? Go on!"

Aunt Jackie makes a shooing motion with her hand but keeps the other planted firmly on her hip. We both watch as Janae slowly walks over to the far side of the cafeteria.

"What kind of wingman are you?"

I just shoved a couple of fries in my mouth but I manage to mumble, "Ma'am?"

"There was a time I couldn't keep the two of you apart. Now Janae's gone off the rails, acting like she ain't got the sense she was born with, and where are you?"

That's the thing about grown-ups—they think kids don't pay attention but they can be just as clueless sometimes. Janae and I haven't been tight for a while now. But I have to say something so I just state the obvious: "I'm right here, Aunt Jackie."

She sighs and closes her eyes. I study her fake eyelashes for a second but then Aunt Jackie's eyes snap back open and she hisses, "Back her up, Taj!"

I carry my tray over to where Marshall's sitting—in No Man's Land. I sit here, too, some days. It's where you go when you just want to be left alone—or when you got no other choice. Marshall's kind of a loner but now he's got Janae standing over him and half the kids in the cafeteria are watching to see what happens next.

"Hey, y'all," I say before setting my tray down and sliding onto the bench a few feet away from Marshall. He grins at me but Janae just gives me the evil eye. She loves being the center of attention but I guess Janae doesn't want a witness to this particular performance.

"What?" I ask innocently.

Janae glances over her shoulder and then quickly turns back to us when she sees her aunt is still standing by the cafeteria door.

"So, Marshall...I just wanted to make sure you were okay after what happened yesterday. I mean, those girls can be brutal, and—"

Janae presses her lips together. When her eyes meet mine, I nod so she knows she's heading in the right direction. Janae takes a deep breath and lets her words spill out. "I should have told them to quit. We've been friends a long time and I should've had your back and...I'm sorry."

Marshall smiles at the lone fish finger on his plate. "It's okay, Janae. I mean, we haven't really hung out since fifth grade. People change. I know *I've* changed."

Marshall tries to laugh but he's still looking at his lunch. His colorful bangs hide his face but they can't hide the ache in his voice. Actually, Marshall doesn't just sound hurt—he sounds *guilty*. Like getting hounded by a bunch of hyenas is somehow *his* fault.

Janae must have heard it, too, because she starts tugging at her long bronze braids like she wishes the curtain would close so she could rush offstage. Her apology hasn't made things better because even though she's not the only kid at our school who picks on Marshall, being cruel to someone who used to be a friend doesn't just make her a bully—it makes her a traitor.

Just when I think she's about to bolt, Janae slides onto the bench across from me and Marshall.

"My aunt says people don't change, though a lot of us try to run away from who we really are." She pauses and looks straight at Marshall. "She thinks that's what I'm doing—trying to be someone I'm not. You've never done that."

The respect in Janae's voice surprises me and embarrasses

Marshall. He laughs shyly and this time it sounds genuine. The three of us have known each other since kindergarten. Back then, Marshall used to be this clean-cut kid—a bit of a nerd and definitely the teacher's pet. Then in third grade he started growing locks and by seventh grade, they were swinging down his back.

You could tell Marshall was proud of his long hair—maybe even a little vain. But then one day he cut most of it off and started adding different colors. Today Marshall's got two ponytails. He pulls his chin-length locks back with elastic bands and lets the ones in front fall into his eyes. Some are blue and some are pink.

I think it's cool to express yourself but Marshall goes a bit too far sometimes. He wore a skirt to school once and he wears earrings, too—in both ears. Not like a tiny gold hoop or a diamond stud—even I've got one of those. Marshall wears long dangly earrings that look like they came from his mother's jewelry box. And he doesn't just wear them to school. I saw him wearing them at a Friday night football game!

Marshall's fashion experiments don't make sense to me, but I'm trying *not* to draw attention to myself. I can't afford to act out or take risks and, to tell the truth, I'm not that brave. But Marshall—he must be fearless. Or foolish. Or maybe being himself just means that much to him.

Aunt Jackie says Marshall's going through a phase. "The boy's just trying to be provocative." Marshall did go to Junior Prom with Shanté Evans last spring, so maybe Aunt Jackie's right. Problem is, Marshall's refusal to lay low makes him a target in the 'hood. He got jumped last spring and lost a tooth! But when those two jerks came to school the next day, one had a black eye and the other had a fat lip.

Marshall's kind of wiry, but he plays tennis so he's fit. Maybe that's why I like him. Marshall will surprise you because he never does what you expect him to do. And no matter what you think of his sense of style, Marshall always goes down swinging.

"So who are you going to choose for the biography project?" I ask.

Janae groans. "I can't believe we have to pick our subject already. The final project isn't due until Thanksgiving."

"Mr. Muhammad doesn't want us all choosing the same person," Marshall explains. "This way at least we know we've got someone all to ourselves."

I loudly slurp the last of my chocolate milk from the carton and then burp to get a rise out of Janae. These days everything I do seems to gross her out.

"I bet half the class is going to choose Martin Luther King," I predict, "and the other half's going to choose Colin Kaepernick."

"The guys might do that, but not the girls," Janae says confidently.

"Who's on your short list?" Marshall asks.

Mr. Muhammad made us pick three contenders. Tomorrow we'll have to defend our choices in front of the whole class.

Janae leans in like she's about to share a secret. "Beyoncé, Nicki Minaj, and Cardi B," she says with pride.

I can't help it—I bust out laughing. Then I pull my social studies folder out of my book bag so I can remind Janae of the point of the project. "You have to choose someone who has made 'a significant contribution to the struggle for freedom.' If you want to pick a woman, Harriet Tubman's a better choice than Cardi B."

Janae glares at me. "Mr. Muhammad said we had to start by coming up with our own definition of freedom. For Black women, doing what we want to do with our bodies and our voices is a big part of what it means to be free."

"She's right," Marshall says, which earns him a smile from Janae. He blushes and asks me, "Who are you going to choose?"

I shrug and put my folder away. "Maybe Paul Robeson or Octavius Catto."

"No women?"

Truth is, Nelson Mandela was my third choice. But I don't want to look like the sexist jerk Janae thinks I am so instead I say, "Well, if *I* put a woman on my list, it'd be someone classy like Marian Anderson."

Janae rolls her eyes. "That so *obvious*. And you just proved my point, Taj. Black women are always pitted against one another—classy ladies versus THOTs. *You* don't get to decide who's worthy of attention."

I ignore her and turn to Marshall. "Who's on your short list?"

"Munroe Bergdorf, Terence Nance, and Prince."

Janae nods like she approves of all three. I'm not so sure. The only person I can picture in my mind is a short dude wearing a frilly lace collar and high-heeled boots.

"Prince? As in 'We're gonna party like it's 1999?'"

Marshall nods and then flips open his notebook to a page covered in doodles. "Look at this symbol. Prince designed it to represent love beyond male and female."

I look at the strange drawing. It looks kind of like a wonky ankh. For the Ancient Egyptians, the ankh was a symbol of life. At least that's what Kwame told me. He sells amulets and hats and t-shirts on 52nd Street.

"I'm trying to design a symbol of my own," Marshall explains. "Prince Rogers Nelson was so ahead of his time. He's just..." Marshall closes his eyes and sighs, "...everything."

When Marshall's eyes open again, he sees we're not as impressed.

"Come on, you two—the man's a legend."

"*Was* a legend," I say. "Didn't he OD?"

Marshall shakes his head. "That was tragic but true legends never die."

I glance at Janae. She's looking at Marshall like he just said something deep. I'm wondering how Marshall's going to defend his choice of a drug addict to Mr. Muhammad.

The bell rings and we get up from the table. Aunt Jackie must have been satisfied because she's nowhere to be seen.

Marshall grabs his tray and says, "I'm working on a video montage for my presentation. To understand Prince's genius, you really have to see him perform."

Janae's eyes grow wide. "Did Mr. Muhammad say it's okay to use tech?"

Marshall nods. "I'm just about done with my presentation. If you want, I could help you put together something for your three artists."

Janae squeals and grabs Marshall by the shoulders. He struggles to keep the trash on his tray as she hops around, but Marshall clearly appreciates Janae's excitement. I watch them and wonder how they can look like best friends when fifteen minutes ago Janae had to be forced to apologize for bullying him.

"OMG—that would be so awesome! Want to meet at the library after school?

"Actually, I have better tech at home," Marshall replies. "You can come over. You, too, Taj. My mom won't mind."

Janae stops jumping up and down and turns to me. The sour look returns to her face and one of her hands settles on her hip. "You coming?"

"I want to but I have to walk Freddie," I tell her.

Janae holds her hand up to my face. "Whatever, Taj," she says, rolling her eyes and stalking off.

Marshall gives me a sympathetic smile as we head out of the cafeteria. "Freddie's your dog?"

I shake my head. "My job."

Marshall dumps his trash into the can and sets his tray on the cart. "Well, it'll take a while to work on Janae's presentation. You can still come by if you want—after you've dropped Freddie off."

"Really?"

"Sure," Marshall says with a smile.

Just then Mike Avery walks by and purposely slams his shoulder into Marshall. Luckily his hand flies out just in time to stop Marshall from going head first into the cafeteria wall. I grip my tray so hard I think the plastic might break. What I really want to do is shatter it completely by hitting Mike over the head as hard as I can. But that would mean a trip to the principal's office and a call home to Mama. Not to mention the fact that Mike and his boys would probably pulverize me.

"Here—give it here. I'll take it."

I look up and realize Marshall is trying to pull the tray out of my hands. I exhale and let go. When I look down at my hands, they're shaking so I shove them into my pockets.

"You alright?" Marshall asks after dumping my trash in the can.

I take a deep breath and try to calm down. "Yeah. You?"

Marshall grins at me and I see the hole where his tooth got knocked out.

"It's cool—he's a friend."

My doubt must show because Marshall laughs and gives my shoulder a squeeze.

"Really—it's okay. Listen, I got to go. I'll see you after school. You know where I live, right?"

I nod and watch as Marshall weaves through the packed hall, multi-colored head held high.

3.

Most days when I'm walking Freddie, we take the outer path at The Woodlands. The inner road is paved, though the asphalt's cracked in a lot of places. Soft green moss grows in the potholes, and once in a while a car goes by but most are parked while people visit graves. On the outer path, the grass has been worn away to dirt and you just have to watch you don't trip over the exposed tree roots.

When I need to think stuff through, that's where we go. Aside from the occasional passing train, it's real quiet out there, which makes it easy to forget that the city's hustling and bustling on the other side of the fence. Freddie trots along beside me or chases after a gutsy squirrel, and I let my mind sort through all the junk I seem to pick up during an average day.

The dirt path passes behind Section K and that's where Kev is buried. By the time I get there today, I've worked up a sweat. The crisp brown leaves on the ground tell me that fall is almost here, but the sun overhead disagrees. I take my coat off and set it on the grass before plunking down next to Kev's grave.

I take a moment to put everything in order. No point complaining to the dead, so I always try to start with good news if I've got any.

"Hey, Kev. I aced that Spanish test today."

I used to pause and wait for Kev reply—at least I'd imagine what he might say. "Handle your business, lil' man. Make your mama proud. In school, outta school—always do your best."

Then he'd palm my head the way you palm a basketball. That was back when I was little. My head's too big for that now.

"Mama got dressed today," I say next.

That's always a good thing. Usually I cook dinner—wieners and beans, Hamburger Helper—and leave a plate out for Mama covered in foil. Late at night, after I've gone to bed, I'll hear her shuffling around the kitchen in her bathrobe and slippers. Sometimes she goes back to bed after she's eaten, but sometimes she stays up and watches TV. We've got premium cable thanks to Juan. He knew a guy who knew a guy and hooked us up with a free box after Kev died. Mama made me thank Juan and it was cool having so many channels at first. But now Mama spends hours glued to the TV and I can't help feeling like Juan's been more of a curse than a blessing when it comes to my family.

Today when I went into the kitchen to get myself some breakfast, I found Mama standing by the stove making scrambled eggs. She'd showered and changed into the pretty teal tracksuit I got her for Christmas last year. The velour's a little baggy now but it still looks good on her, and that's what I told Mama. Then I checked the pill box on the counter to make sure she'd taken her medication.

"You want toast?" she asked.

I nodded and checked the fridge. Only the tough ends of the loaf were left in the bag. When Mama saw me checking them for mold before I put them in the toaster, she opened the freezer and took out a bag of hamburger buns instead.

"Put one of these in the microwave for a few seconds."

The buns were a whole lot older than the loaf of bread in the fridge, but freezer burn is better than mold so I did like she said. Mama found a lone slice of processed cheese in the fridge and a packet of salsa in the catch-all drawer, which made a pretty decent breakfast sandwich.

"Going out today?" I asked after I'd cleaned up the kitchen.

Mama shrugged and peered out the window. She frowned at the blue sky like it couldn't be trusted and said, "Maybe. We need a few things around the house."

We need a *lot* of things around the house. I started to make a list but now I just focus on getting the stuff that really matters. Like fresh milk so I can have cereal for breakfast (and sometimes for dinner, too). I wanted to stay and keep talking to Mama but I had to leave for school. Plus talking too much wears her out. So I gave her a big hug and left knowing Mama probably wouldn't leave the house at all and would be back in her ratty robe and back in bed by the time I got home.

I don't tell all of that to Kev. I pick out the good parts instead. "Mama's taking her medication. Can't really tell if it's working yet, but at least she's giving it a try."

Mama didn't want to see a therapist and she didn't want to go on anti-depressants either. But Mrs. Donovan, our caseworker, gave her an ultimatum: "Take care of your mental health or be declared an unfit parent."

That really hit home. Mama didn't want folks thinking she was crazy but it was worse having people think she was a bad mother. Still, Mama missed her last appointment with her therapist. Each one is written on the calendar we got from the Chinese takeout place, so I always know when they're coming up. Mrs. Donovan knows, too.

Suddenly Freddie starts to whimper. He's a bit skittish sometimes so I just pull him onto my lap and give his belly a reassuring rub. Then I notice that something's changed. The sun is still up in the sky but the air has grown cold. I shiver and glance around. That's when I spot the boy. He's a few rows ahead of me and Freddie, seated on the ground with his knees pulled up to his chest and his back pressed against a tombstone.

I scan Section K but don't see any adults. "Hey," I call out, thinking he might be lost. "You okay?"

The boy's dark eyes open wide. Real wide.

"You playing hide and seek?" I ask with a grin. "Don't worry—I won't give up your secret spot."

For a few seconds the boy just stares at me with his mouth hanging open. Finally he says, "You're not supposed to see me." The boy looks around nervously before adding, "No one ever sees me."

The kid looks like he's about to panic and that's when I notice his funny clothes. He almost looks like he's wearing pajamas but the rough fabric doesn't look like anything I'd want to sleep in. He almost looks like a little prisoner but it's too early to be dressing up for Halloween.

"You must be good at hiding. Are your folks around here somewhere?" When he frowns, I ask my question another way. "Did you come here with your mom and dad?"

A shadow crosses his face and he looks down at his feet. One is turned at an angle that looks uncomfortable.

"I'm an orphan," he says softly.

Freddie whimpers again but I just tuck him under my arm and get to my feet. I pick up my coat and walk over to the sad little boy.

"You're here by yourself—for real?"

The boy nods but then catches himself. "Well—Cin's here, too. But she likes to walk and I can't always keep up."

He reaches for a stick on the grass that I didn't notice before. A small block covered in leather is attached to one end and I realize it's a crutch.

"I have to stop and rest every so often," the boy explains, "but Cin just keeps going around and around..."

"And Sin is...your friend?" I ask.

The boy nods eagerly. "We came here together when they woke

us up."

That doesn't make sense to me, but I'm glad this strange kid has someone looking after him. Plenty of folks jog in the cemetery so maybe that's what he means.

"Is she running on the dirt path?"

The boy thinks for a moment and then slowly shakes his head.

"N-no. Cin follows a path only she can see."

I frown. "And you wait here until she's done?"

The boy nods. "I like it here. It's quiet."

"I like it here, too," I tell him. "I come three times a week, but I've never seen you before."

"No one sees me."

That's the second time he's said that. I shiver and set Freddie down so I can put my coat back on. Freddie cautiously sniffs the grass around the boy's feet, which surprises me. This dog doesn't usually respect other people's boundaries.

"Think your dog can smell me?" asks the boy.

"Sure. Dogs have a really strong sense of smell."

The boy tugs at his ankles, keeping his feet out of reach. But the shine in his eyes tells me he's not afraid.

"You can pet him if you want," I say. "Freddie loves a good belly rub."

That brings a smile to his face. But when the boy keeps his hands clamped around his ankles, I squat down and give Freddie the belly rub he was hoping for.

"I had a dog once," he tells me with a shy smile, "but Matron chased him away. She said he'd bring fleas into the almshouse. We already have lice—bedbugs, too."

"Almshouse? What's that?" I ask. It doesn't sound like any place I'd want to be.

The boy watches Freddie loll on the grass and finally reaches out a hand. But instead of petting the dog, he uses his fingertips to trace the outline of Freddie's tail.

"The almshouse is where all the paupers go. And the orphans. And the lunatics. And cripples like me."

A kid his age would only call himself that if he heard other folks saying it, too. I didn't appreciate our neighbors poking their noses in our business but I'm starting to think this kid might need help. I take a closer look at the boy's clothes. They definitely look like the kind of cheap gear the government would hand out. Maybe he's talking about some type of group home. I've heard stories about those places. That's why I have to fix Mama. If she gets any worse, a group home is where I might end up.

"What's this place called?" I ask.

"Blockley," he says without looking me in the eye.

A lot of apartment complexes have names, but I've never heard of one by that name. "Is it close by?"

"Blockley used to be on the river, but it's not there anymore."

"So...where do you live now?"

"Here."

"*Here*? With...Sin?"

The boy nods again but his eyes are locked on Freddie. His fingers hover just above the dog's fur. He sighs and says, "He's so warm."

Freddie is warm, but I'm not. Despite having my coat on, I shiver violently and turn to find a woman walking towards us. Actually she almost seems to glide over the ground because her long dress hides her feet. It's made from the same striped fabric as the boy's clothes. The two don't look like they're related, but they definitely look like they came from the same place. I hear the word echo in my mind: *Blockley*.

It's hard to tell from this distance but the way she holds herself makes me think the woman's taller than me. She weaves around the tombstones in her path without once taking her eyes off mine. She is already speaking despite the distance between us, and somehow I can hear every word. It's almost like I'm reading her lips or that the wind is carrying her thoughts directly to me.

"The one you love is no longer here. He chose another path. The time has come for you to choose yours. I know what you seek. A way can be found to every world. Just return to me what is mine..."

The boy looks up at me and then peers around the grave to see what has turned me to stone. When he sees the woman, his face changes too.

"I better go," he says with regret. With a quick hop, he gets to his feet, tucks his crutch under his arm, and makes his way toward the woman. He moves quickly with a smooth, swinging motion but turns to say, "Promise you'll come back?"

The Woodlands isn't a scary place. You're even allowed to have a picnic here. They hold special events on the weekends and even show movies sometimes. There's an annual Halloween party for little kids and actors put on plays in Hamilton's old mansion. I've never been afraid here, not even after the sun's gone down. But the dark woman gliding through the graves has got me fighting the urge to run. Freddie starts whimpering again and he's frantically circling my feet. I want to flee but it feels like I'm anchored to the ground. Only it's not the dead holding onto me—it's Sin.

"Promise?"

The boy's desperate plea somehow breaks her spell.

"I promise," I tell him before scooping Freddie up and hurrying toward the front gate. The paved road slopes downward and I'm walking so fast I overtake an elderly jogger. I don't want to but feel compelled to look over my shoulder. I see the woman moving toward the boy with her hand outstretched. She strokes his face and together they weave through the graves until they're out of sight.

As soon as we pass through the cemetery gates, Freddie starts acting like his usual self again. A passing student kicks a prickly chestnut and Freddie howls as the nut rolls by. The soft clang of the trolley's bell reassures me somehow. The air feels warm again and with the setting sun in my eyes, I let Freddie guide me home.

4.

Mrs. Whitmore is sitting in her favorite armchair with a blanket spread across her legs and headphones clamped over her ears. I know because she's in the study. Three of its walls are made of small square panes of glass and there are no curtains to keep out prying eyes. Mrs. Whitmore doesn't seem to mind if her neighbors and anybody walking by can see what she's doing. The wall behind her is covered with books but Mrs. Whitmore prefers to listen to audio books.

I tap on the window to get her attention and then let Freddie wiggle through the dog flap in the side door. He immediately settles at his owner's feet, and she reaches down to pat his head after unfastening his leash. They've only got each other in that great big house, but they seem happy. I wave to Mrs. Whitmore and head to Marshall's place, which is just a couple blocks over.

Kids who live in this neighborhood don't usually go to my school. It's just a ten-minute walk from here, but it feels like a whole other world. Here the streets are lined with massive trees and the Victorian duplexes have brightly painted porches, tinkling wind chimes, and colorful stained glass windows. On my block, we have a few trees but all the yards aren't perfectly landscaped and some of the porches sag or have peeling paint. The only other kid I know around here is Ethan. He's White and we met over the summer when he was mowing lawns. I'd never seen an old-fashioned lawnmower like the one he was using, so I stopped to watch him for a minute. Ethan asked me if I wanted to give it a try.

"It's eco-friendly," he explained. "Totally manual, no fossil fuels, no noise pollution. I turn the clippings into compost, which folks can use in their gardens."

Ethan told me plenty of folks wanted to hire him but he could only cut grass after he got home from robotics camp so he had to turn a lot of jobs down.

"Sounds like you need a partner," I told him. He hired me on the spot.

Everything was great until one day I showed up to do a job and my customer's neighbor called the police. I guess she was used to seeing Ethan with the mower and figured I didn't belong there. It wasn't her lawn so I'm not sure why she was so upset. But the cops showed up, saw me mowing the grass, and just looked at each other. One of them cursed under his breath and told me to sit on the curb while the other one went across the street to talk to the nosy neighbor. She was standing on her front step with her arms folded across her chest. I couldn't hear what she was saying but the cop finally came back over and told me I had to leave.

The customer wasn't home so I just called Ethan and told him to come and get the mower. Next thing I know, Ethan's mother comes storming down the block wearing the same look Aunt Jackie gets when she's fired up. First she cursed out the cops, putting her finger right in their red faces. Then she went across the street and called the nosy lady a racist you-know-what. The cops didn't do anything, even when Ethan's mom took pictures of their badges and patrol car. But as soon as they drove off, she burst into tears and wrapped her arms around me saying, "I'm so, so sorry" over and over again.

Ethan called me the next day and told me his mother posted "the incident" on the block association listserv. Most of their neighbors were so outraged by the way I was treated that eight new customers signed up and requests for our services were still coming in. "You're good for business," Ethan said.

I never told Mama what happened but I put the extra money I earned in the account she opened for me at the credit union. I really wanted to buy the new Xbox but Mr. Jackson said it was better to invest in something that would appreciate over time.

"You can always pawn gold," he told me. But he died before we got a chance to pick out a nice chain for Mama.

When I reach Marshall's place, I stand at the foot of the porch steps for a full minute trying to decide what to do. It's late and part of me just wants to go home. The other part of me hopes that Janae is long gone because hanging out with Marshall for a while could be fun. And I do need to work on my social studies presentation. I finally climb the stairs and ring the bell but the smile slides off my face when Marshall's mother opens the front door and I hear Janae's wild laughter coming from upstairs.

"Go on up," Mrs. Sanders tells me. "Dinner will be ready in about half an hour."

Whatever she's cooking sure smells good, but I didn't tell Mama I'd be out for dinner. She probably hasn't even noticed that I haven't come home from school yet, but I still feel guilty. When I reach the top of the stairs, Marshall sticks his head out of his room and waves me down to the end of a long hallway lined with bookshelves.

"Hey, man—you made it. We're almost done with Janae's presentation but Mom thinks we should stop for supper. My dad's chili is pretty good. Can you stay?"

Before I can answer, Janae starts talking into her phone. She's yelling, actually, which makes me think she must have called Aunt Jackie at her salon. When the hair dryers are going, it's pretty loud in there.

"We *are* working!" Janae winks at Marshall and he stifles a laugh before sinking into a giant beanbag in one corner of the room. "We're almost done but Mrs. Sanders invited us to stay for dinner." Janae's eyes slide to mine. "Taj's here, too," she adds and then, to my surprise, hands me the phone.

"Hi, Aunt Jackie."

Her voice booms through the phone, forcing me to hold it away from my ear. Janae snickers before launching herself onto Marshall's big bed. She flips through a magazine and acts like she's been in Marshall's room a hundred times before.

I try to focus on what Aunt Jackie is saying as my eyes do an inventory: turntables, digital piano, tablet, smartphone, and the biggest monitor I've ever seen is on Marshall's desk. If I had a room like this, I'd never leave home!

"I'm so glad you're finally getting out of the house, Taj. You need to spend more time with kids your age. And don't you worry about your mother—I'll stop by and make sure she's got something to eat. You just enjoy yourself and get your homework done and tell Janae to call me when you two are ready to come home. And be sure you thank Mrs. Sanders for inviting you."

"Yes, ma'am." I hand the phone back to Janae. She stares at me and says, "You're really going to stay?"

I set my book bag on the floor and perch on the edge of the bed. My heart is racing but I try to act cool. "Sure. Your aunt says to call her when we're ready to leave."

"Want to see what we've got so far?" Marshall asks, heaving himself out of the bean bag.

Before I can answer, his father appears at the open door. "Food first! Then you can finish working on your projects. Marshall, show your friends where they can wash their hands."

Their bathroom is bigger than my bedroom. I use a lot of soap and take my time washing up because I don't want to leave a grimy fingerprint in this perfect house. I glance at Janae in the mirror to see if she's nervous, too, but she seems to feel right at home. I've been inside her house plenty of times and it is *nothing* like Marshall's home. But Janae isn't freaking out like I am. It doesn't seem to bother her that every room looks like something out of a magazine—not luxurious, just orderly and clean. Everything matches. Nothing looks out of place. The art on the walls looks like it comes from a museum. I take a deep breath and follow Janae and Marshall downstairs.

Dinner is delicious: vegan chili, kale salad, and homemade cheese biscuits. I want to ask if Mr. Sanders does the cooking every night. I want to know if they always have dinner as a family—in the dining room, not standing at the kitchen counter or sitting on the sofa in front of the TV. I wonder what it would be like to come home to this kind of family day after day after day. I wonder what Marshall would say if he ever came over to my house and saw how different my life is.

I don't say much during dinner but I eat everything on my plate and remember to wipe my mouth with the linen napkin when I'm done. I help clear the table and offer to wash the dishes but Mrs. Sanders shoos me out of the kitchen.

"Who wants ice cream?" she asks.

When I decline, Janae scowls at me. "Relax, Taj. The food is free."

My cheeks burn but I force myself to crack a smile. "I'm lactose-intolerant. You *really* don't want me to have a bowl of ice cream. It could get ugly."

Janae groans and says, "TMI, Taj."

Marshall just laughs. "Dairy does the same thing to me—and Dad. We've got coconut milk ice cream, right, Mom?"

"Why don't you see what's in the freezer?" Mrs. Sanders suggests. Then she places a hand on my arm and says, "It's very considerate of you to think of others, Taj. Some people, who shall remain unnamed, just eat whatever they want and don't think about anyone else."

Mr. Sanders pretends to be hurt by his wife's pointed remark. "I always crack a window, don't I? That's considerate."

I can't remember the last time I laughed so much. I'm not totally relaxed, but with a full belly I no longer feel as anxious as before. The Sanders either don't know about my situation at home, or they know enough about my family to realize I'd rather not answer any questions.

After we clear the table and helped to load the dishwasher, Marshall, Janae and I head back upstairs to his room. Janae throws herself across the bed but I sit on the floor. Marshall's got a lot of expensive stuff in his room and I don't want to risk breaking anything.

"Thanks for doing this, Marshall," I say as I unzip my book bag and take out the notes I've made for my biography project.

"You can come over anytime," Marshall says. "My folks are probably downstairs drinking champagne. Their misfit child has not one but TWO real friends!"

"Your folks are pretty great," I tell him.

Marshall nods. "I totally lucked out. Would have been nice to have some siblings, though."

Janae groans. "I'd give anything to be an only child—and have my own room with no bratty twins breaking stuff and getting into everything. You never have to share. And you even have a lock on your door!"

"It get lonely sometimes," Marshall says. "If I had a brother or sister, I'd have an automatic friend for life."

I feel Janae's eyes on me and know she's waiting to see if I'm going to talk about Daquan. I don't really want to talk about my half-brother down in Texas because that means talking about my dad. He never married my mom, but he married this other lady and started a new family with her. He only calls once a year on my birthday, so I change the subject and get us talking about something else.

"You guys ever heard of a place around here called Blockley?"

They both shake their heads.

"Why?" Marshall asks.

"I met this kid at the cemetery today." I pause and wonder if it's wise to share the strange encounter. I could wait and go to the library tomorrow but Marshall's computer is just a few inches away. I take a deep breath and say, "He told me that's where he lives."

"I'll Google it," Marshall says, typing onto his keyboard. Then he turns the giant monitor so I can see what the search produces. "Looks like you've got two options: Blockley Township and Blockley Almshouse."

"Click on the second one," I tell him. Janae has lost interest and gone back to her magazine, but I shift on the floor to get closer to Marshall's desk. The screen changes in an instant and pulls up a Wikipedia page. Marshall skims the entry and reads out the important bits.

"Looks like it was a hospital and home for the poor. There were 'four sizable buildings including a poorhouse, a hospital, an orphanage, and an insane asylum.'"

Marshall must see the shock on my face because he asks, "What's wrong?"

"That's just what the kid said! 'Paupers, orphans, lunatics, and cripples.'"

Janae looks up long enough to glare at me and say, "You shouldn't talk about the mentally ill that way. Or disabled people."

"Actually, 'crip' has been reclaimed by some activists," Marshall says. "Ever heard of Krip-Hop Nation? They're this radical community of musicians. They fight police brutality, ableism—all - isms. You should check them out."

Janae's already looking it up on her phone. I don't have a data plan on my phone so I say, "I meant no disrespect—that really is how the kid talked."

Janae lets out an exasperated sigh and sets her phone down on the bed. "What kid?"

"The boy I met at The Woodlands today. I thought he must have been making it up."

Janae closes her magazine and props herself up on her elbow. "Hold up—why was there a little kid hanging around the graveyard?"

I can't really answer that so I just shrug. "He said he was an orphan but then this lady showed up. He said they both came from Blockley." I decide to leave out the fact that he called her Sin.

Before any more questions tumble out of Janae's mouth, I ask one of my own. "Marshall, when did Blockley Almshouse open?"

He scans the screen for a moment and replies, "Well, the Philadelphia Almshouse opened in the 1730s, but then it moved to Blockley Township and changed its name in 1835."

"And it's still operating?" Janae asks skeptically.

Marshall squints at the screen and then shakes his head. "Nope. Looks like it morphed into the Philadelphia General Hospital and closed in 1977."

None of us says anything for a moment. Then Marshall smirks and says, "You know what this means, right?"

"What?" I ask, dread churning the chili in my belly.

"Either the kid you met was lying or...he's a ghost!"

They both crack up but I can't bring myself to join in. "There has to be some other explanation. He was a sweet kid. And the woman— she was dressed up."

Janae sighs. "People generally dress up for funerals, Taj."

"Not like this. Her dress was...old. *Real* old."

"Maybe she was part of some historical society," Marshall suggests. "You know those history buffs who do reenactments at all the historic sites around Philly? Or maybe she worked at The Woodlands. Sometimes when you tour a museum, the guide will wear a costume from another era."

Both of those ideas are reasonable but somehow they don't ring true.

When I don't respond, Janae gets impatient. "Did this woman *say* anything to you?"

"Nothing that made any sense. She said she knew what I was looking for and could show me the way to another world."

Janae's eyes open wide. "Uh—that is totally creepy. Maybe she belongs to some kind of cult!"

I give a half-hearted laugh and admit, "I was a little freaked out. Part of me wanted to run but the other part of me..." I didn't mean to share that much so I just give another weak laugh and shut up.

Janae seems ready to drop it but Marshall digs his toe into my leg. "What did the other part of you want?"

I shrug and trail my fingers over the plush carpet. "I felt like I couldn't move—but also like I *shouldn't* run. She was coming towards me and she just seemed so..."

Powerful. The word is right there on the tip of my tongue but I swallow it and instead say, "...weird."

Suddenly Janae reaches out and smacks me hard across the back of my head. "Why are you hanging out with some creepy lady in a graveyard, Taj?"

"Ow! Chill, Janae. I wasn't hanging out with her. I was just—"

I don't want to admit that I was talking to my dead uncle so instead I say, "I was walking Freddie. Can I help if it weird people are drawn to me?"

"Well, you know what my aunt always says: 'Like attracts like.' If you want people to think you're normal, you've got to act that way."

I know Janae means that as a diss but Marshall jumps in before I can think of a comeback.

"Why would he want people to think he's normal?" Marshall asks. His face is serious but there's a hint of mischief in his voice. "Are you normal, Taj?"

I chuckle and say, "I think I used to be but...not anymore. Now I talk to ghosts in the cemetery."

"Being normal's overrated," Marshall says.

Janae grunts and says, "Everyone can't afford to be a free spirit, you know."

I'm used to Janae turning on me for no apparent reason, but Marshall looks totally surprised.

"What do you mean?" he asks.

Janae does a sweep of the room with her arm. "Look at this place! You can explore your identity all you want because your parents aren't going to throw you out. Everybody isn't so lucky. My cousin lives down South. He came out to his mother and now he's living on the street."

Marshall gives a somber nods and says, "I hear you. I definitely lucked out with my folks."

I think about Mike Avery and the scene in the cafeteria today. "Hold up—Marshall may have a nice house and cool parents but that doesn't mean he's got it easy."

"I never said that, Taj. I'm just saying people pay a price for being different. And some people pay more than others."

"What's your cousin going to do?" Marshall asks.

Janae shrugs. "Aunt Jackie told Ty to come live with us but we have a full house already. She's got one sister who's a druggie and another who's a bible thumper. And all us kids just keep landing on her doorstep. It's not fair."

I've never heard Janae talk about her family like that. I guess I've been so worried about Mama that I haven't thought about anyone else having problems, too. Seems like I'm not the only one who could use a way out.

I take a chance and ask, "What if the lady in the cemetery was right? What if there *was* a whole other world where things were better—would you go?"

Janae rolls her eyes at me. "And join some freaky cult? No, thanks."

Marshall looks intrigued. "What are we talking about here—like a parallel universe?"

"I don't know. Maybe. Or a whole other planet out there in the universe. If they were looking for volunteers to go to Mars, I might sign up. We've pretty much messed up Earth."

"The grass is always greener, Rocket Boy. If humans messed up Earth, why wouldn't they do the same thing to Mars? This is the only home we've got. It's the only home we deserve."

I hate to admit it, but Janae's probably right. There's no way out.

For a while we just sit there in silence. Then Marshall perks up and says, "Hey, want to see something cool?"

We nod and draw closer to his desk. Marshall clicks on an icon and the screen transforms. In the middle of a room that looks identical to the one we're in is a digital version of Marshall.

"Is that...you?" I ask.

Marshall nods. "It's my avatar. I used to be really into VR." Marshall taps his keyboard and the screen splits from one scene to four. Everything is painted in neon colors but I recognize every place: the cafeteria, the science lab, and the basketball court outside our school.

"I didn't know you could code," Janae says, clearly impressed.

"My godmother taught me. I used to spend hours in here, glued to the computer. I figured if I didn't belong in the real world, I could design one that was better. No bullies, no binaries, no b.s."

Janae nods like that makes sense to her, which makes me want to swallow my question. But then I see that familiar smirk and I know she knows that I don't know what Marshall's talking about. So I ask, "What's that second one?"

"Binaries? You know, the way everything gets split in two. You're either this or that—male or female, White or Black, gay or straight, punk or thug."

"Virgin or ho," Janae inserts.

Marshall nods. "A single box can't cover all of who we are but we're only allowed to check one."

I take a closer look at the four scenes. Some of the virtual kids I recognize from school. Then I see one tall kid who's been given a special makeover. "Is that Mike Avery?"

Marshall grins. "Yep—in living color."

In the virtual world, Mike isn't some basketball goon who slams Marshall into the cafeteria wall for kicks. Instead he looks like Marshall's twin. In matching outfits they eat lunch in the cafeteria, dance together in Marshall's bedroom, and shoot hoops in the schoolyard. When Mike hits a three-point shot, it isn't Keysha who storms the court to throw her arms around him—it's Marshall.

Janae laughs so hard that tears stream down her cheeks and before long she's coughing and gasping for air. When Janae finally stops wheezing, she holds up her phone to take a picture of virtual Mike but Marshall slaps her phone away from the screen.

"Don't. I promised him I wouldn't show anyone."

"Wait—are you saying Mike *knows* about this?" I ask.

"Sure. He comes over sometimes."

Janae's mouth falls open. I'm just as shocked but then I remember what Marshall said earlier today. "So...you really *are* friends with Mike Avery?"

Marshall nods and with one click of the mouse, makes the vibrant, dancing digital version of himself disappear.

"Why keep his secret?" I ask.

"Like Janae said, freedom comes at a cost. Everybody can't afford to be open about who they are—or want to be."

I feel sorry for Janae's cousin but it's hard to have much sympathy for a jerk like Mike. If the way he is at school really is just an act, it's pretty convincing. Then again, I've got everybody fooled. Maybe the Mike Marshall knows is the real deal. Maybe that neon virtual world is the only place Mike can be his true self. Everybody needs a place like that.

I start thinking about the cemetery again. It used to be a place where I felt safe. But after what happened there today…I'm not sure I want to go back.

Mrs. Sanders knocks and sticks her head into the room. "Are you kids almost done with your homework? It's getting late. I think you better wrap up so I can drive you home."

"I'm ready to go." Janae slides off the bed and grabs her book bag. She cozies up to Marshall's mom and disappears with her down the hall.

I look at the pinball screensaver on Marshall's giant monitor. "How long did it take you to build that other world?"

"Over a year," Marshall tells me. "I was so into it that I hardly left my room last summer. Then my godmother reminded me that she taught me to code so I would change the real world, not hide from reality."

"How can you change the world by coding?" I ask.

"Look at social media. There are so many platforms and apps— it's totally changed the way we interact with each other. There are a bunch of apps that let homeless teens connect with allies who can offer them a place to stay or something to eat."

"That would definitely help Janae's cousin."

"Yeah. And a whole lot of LGBTQ kids. Queer kids of color are more likely than other teens to wind up homeless."

I want to ask Marshall which one of those letters describes who he is. But Mr. Jackson always said, "Live and let live," so I decide to mind my business instead.

I grab my book bag and head for the door. "Thanks for having us over, Marshall."

"Sorry we didn't get a chance to work on your presentation," he says apologetically.

"That's okay. I think I'm going to choose Paul Robeson. Mr. Jackson took me to his house last year. It's a museum now. Maybe I can go there and do some research this weekend."

"And there's that dope mural of Robeson on Chestnut and 45th. Maybe we could shoot some footage over there."

"That'd be cool. Thanks, Marshall."

As we head downstairs, Marshall asks over his shoulder, "Are you going to go back to that cemetery?"

"I don't know. Would you?"

Marshall stops on the landing and turns to face me. "Know how you said there was a part of you that didn't want to run away?"

I nod and Marshall puts his hand on my chest.

"My godmother told me that's your intuition—your sixth sense. We ignore it a lot of the time but it's there to guide us. If your gut told you *not* to run, there's a reason. Trust your gut—and stay away from ice cream!" he says with a grin.

I chuckle as I follow Marshall out to the car, but I hardly sleep a wink that night with the woman's clear voice whispering in my ears.

A way can be found to every world. Just return to me what is mine...

5.

For the rest of the week there is no sun, only rain and fog and sullen skies. Mama stays in bed and misses another appointment with her therapist. That means Mrs. Donovan will come soon. While I'm walking Freddie, I try to think of a way to make things right.

I'm not avoiding the cemetery, but I spend a long time in Clark Park throwing Freddie his favorite toy. After a while Freddie gets bored and stops chasing after the slobber-soaked tennis ball. He turns his little body toward Woodland Avenue so I clip his leash back on and let Freddie pull me up the hill.

The red brick walkway is plastered with slick wet leaves. I slip once and use that as an excuse to slow down. My heart is still racing, though, and I can't decide whether I'm afraid to see the strange woman—or eager.

As we pass through the gates, I take a deep breath and decide to stay on the paved road that circles the cemetery. With all this rain, the dirt path will be muddy and Freddie's not wearing his little boots. We get all the way around the cemetery without seeing anyone else. I start to relax but when I reach Section K, I don't have time to say anything to Kev. The boy is waiting for me, his smile warm and bright despite the gloomy weather.

"You came back," he says, sliding off the tombstone he was perched upon.

"I keep my promises," I tell him. Freddie sniffs the ground around the boy's feet but doesn't whimper this time.

"You never told me your name."

"I'm Drew. What's your name?"

"Taj."

"Cin wants to meet you," he says.

My stomach turns over. I think of the woman's dark, piercing eyes and wonder what she has in store for me. I pick up a stick and show it to Freddie. He immediately starts to dance and then tears across the grass when I hurl the stick over the graves.

"How did she get that name?" I ask the boy. "It's…different."

Drew's eyes follow Freddie but he still answers my question.

"Her real name is Lucinda but everyone at Blockley calls her Cin. They're afraid of her."

"I can see why!" I say but then notice the hurt in Drew's eyes. "I mean, Cin is…kind of intimidating."

"She's always kind to me—and she helps many of the other patients, too." He leans in and whispers, "The nurses think Cin's a witch."

"Why do they think that?" I whisper back.

Drew shrugs. "She can do things they can't."

My stomach flips again. I squat down to pull the stick from Freddie's jaws. "Like what?"

Drew glances at me and then kicks at his crutch. The leather part that goes under his arm is worn and he holds it at an angle that suggests it's too long for his small body. A hand-me-down crutch from the fine folks at Blockley.

"I'm not supposed to say," he says quietly.

"It's a secret?"

Drew nods.

There are at least four kinds of people who lived at the almshouse. Cin clearly isn't an orphan, so is she sick? Mentally ill? Or just poor? I'm lost in my thoughts but Drew must think I'm bored with him because he volunteers some information about his strange friend.

"Matron hates Cin, but she's just afraid. The other inmates tell stories, you see, and the nurses believe them even though not all of those stories are true."

"Can you tell me something about Cin—something true?"

Drew looks around to make sure we're alone. "She wasn't born here," he confides.

I lower my voice, too. "In Philadelphia, you mean?"

Drew shakes his head. "In America," he whispers.

I wonder if being an immigrant in the nineteenth century is the same as being an immigrant in the US today. Is Drew ashamed that his friend's a foreigner, or is he afraid she won't be safe if others find out?

"What else can you tell me about Cin?" I ask.

"What is it you want to know?"

The hairs on the back of my neck stand up and Freddie scurries behind me. Drew gives me a reassuring smile and I take a deep breath before turning to face Cin.

She's much smaller than I remembered, and I'm close enough now to see that her black hair is streaked with white. She's an elder but her skin is smooth, which makes me think of how Mama always says, "Black don't crack!" My grandmother hardly had any wrinkles, either. Nana had long silver locks but Cin's tightly coiled hair is parted in the middle and pulled back into a tidy bun. She isn't wearing any makeup or jewelry. Her hands are clasped behind her back.

I swallow hard and try to make my heart slow down. "I—I've been thinking about what you said the other day."

Cin looks pleased, though she doesn't smile. Instead she surprises me by saying, "Walk with me."

She turns and heads for the dirt path. I offer the stick to Drew. "Why don't you play with Freddie for a while?"

Drew stares at the stick and then looks over at Cin. She nods at him over her shoulder as if giving him permission, but Drew still doesn't take the stick from my hand.

"Place it on the ground," Cin tells me.

I do as I'm told. Freddie dances back and forth, eager for someone to toss the stick. Drew squats and stares at the piece of wood. Then he holds out his hand and flicks his wrist without grabbing hold of the stick. To my surprise, it goes flying over the graves and Freddie takes off.

"How did you do that?" I ask Drew.

He just grins, and shrugs, and eagerly waits for Freddie to deposit the stick at his feet. Cin is already heading down the outer path so I hurry to catch up with her. She speaks first, which gives me a moment to catch my breath.

"It has been a long time since Andrew has had something to look forward to. It has been a long time since he's had a friend."

"He has you."

The corners of her mouth dip downward. "My path is my own, and I walk it alone. In life, in death...I have a role to play."

Her words have a sing-song quality that makes me think Cin has said them so many times that she knows them by heart. "Drew told me you helped the other patients at Blockley."

"I did what I could. The botanist allowed me to harvest herbs from his garden—columbine or cranesbill to stop the blood, lavender for the restless, valerian for those unable to sleep."

She pauses to glance at me and I wonder if she can tell I haven't been sleeping well myself.

Cin sighs and says, "I made simple tinctures, teas, and salves.

Nothing more."

"Is that why some folks thought you were a witch?" I ask as respectfully as I can.

This time her full lips twist upward into a strange smile. "People fear what they do not understand. To some, I was a witch. To others, I was a murderer. To those like you," her eyes slides to me once more, "I am an answer to prayer."

I can't remember the last time I prayed. When Nana was alive, I used to go to church with her on Sundays and she taught me to recite some bible verses. But way too much messed up stuff has happened in my life for me to think God's looking out for my family.

Somehow talking to Cin—being chosen by her—makes me feel important. I haven't felt that way in a while.

"How can you help someone like me?" I ask.

"We can help one another, I think."

"*You* need help?"

The surprise in my voice stops Cin in her tracks. "You believe you have nothing to offer?"

What could a kid like me have that a ghost would want? "I guess that depends on what kind of help you need."

Cin starts walking again. "I worked for a woman once—a wealthy White woman. My mistress had...a particular friend. She loved her very much and wanted to elope. But where in this world could they go? Her parents expected her to marry one of the suitors they had chosen for her—men of means and status. So my mistress asked for my help. She knew that I had...a certain gift. This gift was passed to me at birth. My kind has always served yours."

"What's 'my kind?'"

"Seekers are easy to spot. You are searching for something— relief, a reprieve, a way out of a predicament. I have met your kind everywhere—even on the great ship that brought me to this land a lifetime ago."

Her words are clipped, short and sharp-edged like the blades of grass that pass through my mower. "So you're not an immigrant. You're a slave—from Africa!"

"I am no slave. I am Mende," she says with a proud tilt of her chin.

I nod even though I'm not really sure what that means. I've never heard of a country by that name, but there are more than fifty countries on the continent of Africa. I make a mental note to look it up the next time I'm at the library.

"So these seekers—people like me—they were on the slave ship with you?"

"Yes. Many of our people were already defeated. The enslavers broke them with brutal beatings, rape, and starvation. Those who dared to resist were crushed without mercy. But there were others..."

Cin stops walking and gazes toward the distant river. A train rattles along the tracks outside the cemetery and I think of a time when ships carried just as many passengers across the sea. Except my ancestors weren't passengers—they were captives.

"One woman on the ship came from my village. I was just a child but she knew my mother and my mother's mother. She knew I had inherited their gift, so she asked for my help."

For several moments Cin is silent, drifting away with her memories. I wonder what a child could do on a ship in the middle of the Atlantic Ocean. To get Cin talking again I ask, "Did you set her free?"

Cin shakes her head and declares, "She set herself free."

"How?"

"She dove into the sea." Without looking at me, Cin walks away.

I stand there with my mouth open, unsure what to do. Finally I rush after Cin and blurt out, "You told her to jump overboard? But...she must have drowned!"

Cin's face shows no emotion. "The choice was hers to make."

"You said you *helped* her," I insist.

Cin nods. "I did not tell her *what* to do. I simply told her *when*."

I've heard that sharks trailed after slave ships because they knew a meal was guaranteed. It's hard to see how getting devoured by sharks is better than being a slave in America.

Cin reads my silence and says, "If you have questions, I will answer them as best I can."

"That sounds like a horrible way to die. I just—I don't see how what you did helped her."

"You assume she jumped to her death. If that was her intention, she would not have come to me."

I think about that for a moment. "You told her *when* to jump. So...the timing mattered?"

Cin looks pleased again. "You are beginning to understand. There are often risks when moving from one world to another. Sometimes the way is clear. Sometimes it is not."

Maybe Marshall was right when he talked about a parallel universe the other night. I don't think Cin is sending people to Mars. I decide it's best to come clean. "I'm not sure I understand how your gift works."

Cin stops walking and points to the low wall of an enclosed plot. I sit down and spread my palms over the cool marble to steady myself. Cin is a ghost—not a reenactor or the leader of some cult. This can't be real and yet...it *feels* real. I take a deep breath and try to concentrate on her words.

"There are doors that lead from one world to another."

I nod even though I already want to interrupt and ask a question. Cin speaks slowly, calmly, with her dark eyes locked on mine.

"I know when they are nearby and when they are open. That is my gift."

I take a moment to weigh what Cin has said. "So this woman

you helped—she didn't drown in the sea. She passed through an open door? Underwater?

"Yes."

"And...where did she go once she passed through the door?"

"Away."

"Yeah, but...where exactly?"

"I do not have the power to see beyond the threshold. Only those who pass through the door know what lies beyond."

"Well, can they come back? I mean, is it like a one-way trip or..."

Cin frowns. I can't tell if she's confused or offended. I try again.

"It's just that the people you help are taking a really big risk. What if the other world is worse than the one they're leaving behind?"

"Those who ask for my help cannot afford the luxury of doubt. They are resolute. You, too, must be unwavering if you wish to help your mother."

I shiver and shift a bit farther away from Cin. How could she know about Mama? Maybe she overheard my conversations with Kev. Did I ever say I wanted to disappear?

"Are you saying that passing through one of your doors will make Mama better?"

"The injustice of this world is the source of her discontent, her dis-ease. She can be comforted but she cannot be cured."

"But what if the door we go through leads straight to hell?"

"Hell is a fiction. The door is real."

"And these other worlds you talk about—what are they like?"

"I can only tell you what my mother told me. The Almighty created the universe."

"You mean God?"

Cin nods and continues. "The universe is vast. It contains this world and many others."

For some reason the verses Nana taught me start playing in my head. I recite a bit for Cin. "'For God so loved the world, that he gave his only begotten son.' *The* world. *This* world. You're saying He made others?"

Cin looks disgusted but she answers my question anyway. "He? There is no *he*—or *she*. God is God. God is the Creator. We are God's children and many homes have been made for us. We have the power to choose, but many are too scared or too weak to abandon the world they know."

Scared and weak—that pretty much sums up how I feel right now. But my gut is trying to tell me something. I feel a hunger deep inside of me. I need to know just what Cin is offering.

"I could take my mother to another world? And you're saying she would be better there—healthy and happy?"

"I offer no guarantees, only opportunity. The choice is yours and yours alone."

"But you'll show me where the door is?"

Cin shakes her head. "You must find it for yourself. In this condition, my powers are limited. It is close, but I can only tell you when it will open."

"How will I know I've found the right door? What will it look like?"

"It will bear my mark."

Before I can ask another question, Cin turns and heads up the path. "I will give you time to consider my offer."

I'm not ready for this conversation to end. Angry, confused, and desperate I call out, "What do you want from me in return?"

Cin freezes but doesn't turn to face me. Instead she speaks over her shoulder.

"Parts of me are pickled in jars and stored not far from this place. Those parts must be restored to me. I *will* be whole once more.

6.

In science class Ms. Kim tells us that Hurricane Florence has stalled over North Carolina. She says the outer bands are churning up warm air and sending more rain our way. I know all about climate change and everything Ms. Kim says about the hurricane makes sense. But I can't help feeling like Cin has something to do with the change in the weather. Her words hang over me like the dark clouds that have smothered the sun.

It's hard to concentrate in class when I keep hearing a ghost's voice in my head. But I have to stay focused and that's why I don't take the note Janae tries to pass me. That leaves her arm hanging in the space between our rows and that's why she gets caught and not me.

When the bell rings, I don't stick around to face Janae's wrath. But when I reach my block, I see Janae chatting over the fence with my landlord like they're old friends. I don't know how she manages to come up with something to say to everyone, but I know I don't want to hear what Janae's got to say to me.

When Jillian sees me coming, she waves but Janae doesn't miss a beat. She keeps talking like I'm not even worth her attention. I'd love to slip inside and leave them out on the street but Jillian puts her hand on my arm as I pass through the gate.

"How's your mom, Taj? Did she try those drops I gave you?"

I nod. Without words, it feels less like a lie. Mama's already on medication. She can't be taking holistic stuff at the same time, but Jillian's already made it clear that she doesn't trust "Big Pharma." I don't know if doing yoga and eating kale can cure depression, but if it really did work, I think a lot more people would be giving it a try.

I'm no expert but I've done some research online and I know it doesn't help to say things like "stay positive" to someone who's depressed. Mental illness has a lot to do with the chemicals in your brain so thinking happy thoughts just isn't enough.

Jillian moves her hand from my arm to Janae's. "If you want to practice on me, you're welcome to stop by anytime."

"Thanks, Jill," Janae says with a smile. "I've been practicing in front of the mirror at home. The last thing I want is to seem fake during my admissions interview."

Janae's still not looking at me but I know she's talking *to* me. *About* me.

"Well, I'll let you two get started on your homework."

As soon as Jillian turns her back, the fake smile slides off Janae's face. I can't remember the first time I realized Janae was pretty. We've known each other forever but one day she just changed—or maybe I did. I don't know. But it's weird how she can scowl and even cuss at me and not look any less beautiful.

"What's up?" I ask casually even though a wave of heat is creeping up my neck.

Janae's dark eyes sweep over me and her lips twist with contempt.

"You only talk to ghosts now? Or maybe they've been teaching you how to disappear."

I glance over my shoulder to make sure the window to our apartment is shut. I don't need Mama hearing Janae's big mouth talking all kinds of nonsense.

"Sorry about the note, okay? I can't afford to get in trouble right now."

"Who can, Taj? Why are you always trying to be so damn perfect?"

"Why do you think?" I yell, surprised by my own sudden anger. I take a deep breath and lower my voice. "I don't want my mother to worry about me."

"And what about everybody else? Your mother's not the only one who cares, Taj. Besides, it's *her* job to take care of you—not the other way around."

"She can't. Not right now."

Janae looks like she wants to say something sharp but she eats her lips to keep the words inside. A few seconds later she opens her mouth and the tone of her voice has changed completely.

"You ready for your mock interview? We should practice. You know you turn into a block of wood when you're nervous."

I shrug and drop down onto the last step of the stoop. "I haven't given it much thought." That's not really true, but it saves me having another conversation that starts with, "My mother needs me right now."

Janae sinks down beside me and keeps her voice bright. "It's important, you know. This is our chance to get into a really good school. And you have to go to a good high school if you want to get into a good college. I'm hoping I get into Masterman. What about you?"

The sound of plastic clattering to the pavement saves me from having to answer Janae's question. On the sidewalk in front of my house a squirrel freezes, sniffs the air, and then darts back up the maple tree. It leaves on the sidewalk an empty plastic jar of peanut butter.

"No that squirrel did not just try to run up a tree with a jar of

Skippy in its mouth," Janae says.

"It did, too," I say with a smile. Mama hates squirrels but I think they're kind of cute. I mean, the squirrels around here are kind of gangster, but they're still fluffy.

Janae surprises me by jumping up and walking over to the plastic jar. She pulls something from her back pocket and starts sawing at the plastic. I never knew Janae carried a knife. That's the kind of thing that could get her suspended from school or worse if a cop ever decided to stop and frisk her.

Then I think about that time I was at the barber shop and these guys—grown men—started talking about Keysha. I mean, sure—she turns heads when she walks down the street, but Keysha's an eighth grader like me! Last year Aunt Jackie made Mama throw out all her R. Kelly CDs. I didn't really understand why till that day in the barbershop. I don't know what I'd do if I ever heard grown men talking about Janae like that, but I'm glad she's looking out for herself.

"What are you doing?" I ask.

"The squirrel got its teeth through the plastic but all the peanut butter's here at the bottom of the jar. No point trying to haul the whole thing up a tree." She finishes sawing off the bottom of the jar and sets it like a dish at the foot of the tree. Then Janae folds her knife and puts it back in her pocket. She joins me on the steps and we wait to see what will happen.

After a few moments, the squirrel comes down the tree head first. It sniffs at the goopy brown peanut butter and noses the jagged edge of the round plastic plate.

"Go on," Janae urges. "You can do it!"

The squirrel believes her because in a flash it clamps its teeth into the plastic and scurries up the tree with its peanut butter feast.

"Everybody needs a hand once in a while," Janae says.

I nod and we just sit there on the stoop for a while. Behind us,

Jill and Wendy's rainbow flag billows with the breeze. It feels like we've gone back in time, back to when Janae and I were best friends and weren't old enough to worry about family problems or getting into a good school.

I sort of wish I could make this moment last but then this little kid rolls up on a BMX bike that's way too big for him. He stops right in front of us and says to Janae, "That your man?"

Janae rolls her eyes and says, "Get lost, Marvonn."

He ignores her and studies me for a few seconds. Finally he asks, "Your mama crazy?"

Janae starts to heave herself off the step but I put my hand on her arm. You shouldn't let anybody talk about your mama, but he's just a little kid. "Naw," I say.

He nods like he believes me. Then he asks, "You crazy, too?"

I surprise all of us—myself most of all—by laughing out loud. Janae shakes my arm off and lunges at the kid. He hoists himself onto the bike seat and pedals away as fast as he can.

Janae sits back down and says, "Don't listen to him. My aunt calls him 'Marvonn the Mouth.' Six years old and already in everybody's business."

"It's okay. I know folks talk about my mother. After what happened to Kev, they probably wonder if it runs in the family. Sometimes I wonder, too."

"There's nothing wrong with you, Taj."

I shrug. "Not yet. Maybe there's something inside of me that won't come out till I'm older." I don't know why I'm telling this to Janae but it feels good to finally let the words outside of my head. They're less scary floating on the air.

"Some scientists think addiction lives in your genes—not the disease itself but, like, the *potential*."

"What do you think?" I ask.

Janae looks up the block so she doesn't have to look at me. "I'm nothing like my mother. I'm *never* going to be like her."

Hadiyah crosses the street and waves at us as she goes by. She used to babysit us when we were little but now she's got three kids of her own. Hadiyah's dressed in black from head to toe. Her headscarf is long enough to be a blouse, and her long loose skirt almost sweeps the street when she walks. She's wearing black sandals, too, but the striped socks she's got on look like they came from Marshall's neon virtual world.

"Love your funky socks, Hadiyah," Janae says with a smile.

"Thanks, girl," she replies. "You two be good now."

We both chuckle and answer, "We will," in unison just like we used to when we were kids.

Once Hadiyah's out of earshot I ask, "Why do you always talk to people like that?"

Janae frowns. "What do you mean?"

"You talk to everybody, Janae—Mrs. Sanders, my landlady, strangers on the bus. What's up with that?"

For a long while, Janae says nothing. That's how I know I've ruined the good feeling between us.

Finally she says, "Know what your problem is, Taj? You're trying so hard to make people think you're normal that you've forgotten what being normal actually looks like. I talk to people because I'm friendly. I talk to people because I have something to say. I talk to people because having social skills matters. Mrs. Diouf says we have to act like we belong in every room. That means talking to everyone like they're your equal, and finding out what you've got in common. You think you're so different..."

Mrs. Diouf is our guidance counselor. She's been prepping us for our admissions interviews but I haven't paid all that much attention to her advice.

Janae gets up. "You're not the only one with problems, Taj."

"I know that, Janae."

"Then act like it."

Before I can think of anything else to say, Janae tosses her braids over her shoulder and heads down the block.

I sit on the stoop and think about what Janae just said. Then I stand up and pull out my key. I can't go after Janae. I need to check on Mama. If Janae doesn't like my priorities, that's her problem. Not mine.

Even before I let myself into the house I hear Wendy and Jill laughing and singing in their kitchen. I even recognize the song: "I Ain't Never Loved a Man." Since Aretha passed a couple of weeks ago, Mama's been playing a lot of her songs, too.

I head upstairs and try to remember what's left in the cupboard that I can use to make supper. When I reach the kitchen, I find Mama peering inside a round tin Mrs. Whitmore gave me last week.

"What's in here?" Mama asks.

"Scones. Mrs. Whitmore made them."

Mama's forehead wrinkles just a bit, so I rush to remind her about my dog-walking job.

Mama sniffs at the scones. "She feeds you?"

I quickly shake my head. "No, but I told her once how you drink lots of tea and she said maybe you'd like something to go with it. They look kind of dry," I add so Mama will know it's no big deal if she doesn't like them.

"That's why you eat them with cream and jam."

Mama's got that shine in her eye that lets me know she's remembering something—something good. I play along to see if I can get her to share her memory. "Whipped cream—on biscuits?"

"No, silly—clotted cream. It's a bit like cream cheese, but better. Maybe we should have a tea party."

We can definitely get jam at our local grocery store, but I'm not too sure about clotted cream. Mama seems to read my mind because she says, "Of course, we'd have to make our own. I made it once or twice with your Nana. She was always hosting her church friends, and you know how those good Christian ladies liked to outdo one another. Who has the fanciest hat? Who hosts the best coffee hour?"

Mama smiles at the memory. Then she pulls out her phone and looks something up. "It's not that hard to make clotted cream. I know you just got home, Taj, but can you run to the store and get a pint of heavy cream? It'll be in the dairy section, near the eggs."

"Sure, Mama."

I slip my coat back on and head for the door. Mama surprises me by holding out a ten-dollar bill.

"Maybe get some fancy jam, too. All we got in the fridge is grape jelly and God only knows how old that jar is. If we're going to do this, we better do it right."

I stop and take a good look at my mother. She notices me staring and says, "What?" with a hint of attitude.

I blush because in my mind I'm thinking, "You look normal today, Mama." But what I say out loud is, "You look different today, Mama."

"You finally noticed!" she cries, patting her long, skinny locks. "Jackie gave me some tints this time. What do you think?"

"It looks real nice, Mama."

"It's not too red?"

I shake my head. "That color suits you. And it's more wine-colored than red."

Mama walks past me to check her reflection in the bathroom mirror. She has to turn her head sideways for the light above to reveal her highlights. "Subtle, right?"

I nod and stand behind her so I can see what she sees in the mirror. I breathe in the smell of her perfume and try to keep my smile from eating my whole face.

Mama's reflection winks at me and I grin back before taking the money and heading for the store. All the way there and back I think about questions I can ask that will keep Mama talking. It's a big deal that she got dressed and went to the salon today. There's still no food in the house but when I get back we order Chinese, which is fine with me. While Mama pours the cream onto the baking tray, I chomp on an egg roll and tell her about Marshall's strange choice for the biography project.

"Prince *was* ahead of his time," Mama tells me. "That funky symbol—he used it to stand up to his record label. He changed his name, wrote 'SLAVE' on his cheek...that man was something else! I got a few of his albums around here somewhere..."

We don't party like it's 1999, but Mama and I do have a lot of fun over the next few hours. I want to stay up and enjoy the mother I remember, but the cream has to bake in the oven overnight so there's nothing for me to do. Mama insists that I need eight hours of sleep to do my best at school, so I finally give in and go to bed.

Mama doesn't. She stays up all night. I hear her going up and down the stairs, doing load after load of laundry in the basement. In between cycles Mama cleans the entire apartment. I hardly recognize our place when I get up. The bathroom is spotless and the hardwood floors are slippery with lemon-scented wax. Mama's at the table working on a grocery list when I walk into the kitchen. All the moldy and past due food has been thrown into the trash. The fridge has been scrubbed clean but it's still empty.

"I'll get breakfast at school," I say before planting a kiss on Mama's cheek. She nods but barely looks at me and I head to school knowing just what I'll find when I get home.

But Mama surprises me. When I unlock the door, the apartment is dim and quiet. I go into Mama's room expecting to find her under the covers, but she's not there. Instead the bed is covered with clothes. Shoes and handbags are strewn across the floor. It looks like Mama tried on everything in her closet before she went out. Then I take a closer look and realize these are work clothes—blazers and blouses and skirts. The kind of clothes Mama used to wear at the law firm.

My gut tells me something's not right but I get my homework out and try not to look up at the clock. At six I call Aunt Jackie but she hasn't seen Mama since she came by the salon yesterday. Wendy and Jill haven't seen her either so when it starts to get dark, I go out looking for my mother.

When Nana was alive, we all lived together in her house. But when she got cancer, it got hard to make the mortgage payments even with Kev and Mama helping out. Cancer took Nana and then the bank took our house. White people live there now. They got rid of the pretty sky blue paint that made our house stand out, but they kept Nana's rosebushes. Mama says the dark gray color makes it look soulless, but there are more and more houses just like it in our neighborhood.

I go up and down the blocks, looping between 50th and 52nd Streets. I want to run but force myself to walk, to act normal, to hide the panic swelling inside of me. Trains come and go above Market Street and I scan the passengers flowing out of the station even though Mama hasn't worked in months. When I reach Baltimore Avenue, I see a couple of beat cops but know that if I tell them my mother is missing I'll be guaranteed a spot in a group home tonight.

I head north and pass a house that looks like it has vomited its contents into the yard. Its fence has been torn down as well so jagged hunks of timber and shards of broken tile spill onto the sidewalk. A freshly painted door leans against the corner property's side wall, its clear glass knob sparkling in the light cast by the streetlamp. I turn back to get a second look and then trip on a hunk of porcelain from a busted toilet. I steady myself and then fold in half when an invisible fist punches me in the gut. I wheeze, struggle to pull in air, and then find myself sprawled on the pavement.

"You alright, son?"

It takes a few seconds for my eyes to focus. Finally they land on the elderly woman who has stopped pushing her shopping cart along the opposite side of the street. Realizing she's waiting for me to prove that I'm alright, I get up and brush the dust from my knees. Then I wince because my right palm is bloody and I can see at least three splinters embedded in my skin.

"It's a shame the way they've torn up that old house. Hammering away day and night, throwing trash right out the windows, making a mess of the block. A child stepped on a nail just the other day! You tell your mama to get you a tetanus shot, you hear?"

"Yes, ma'am."

I can't tell Mama anything if I can't find her. I wave at the woman with my left hand and slowly move on.

With my palms stinging and my knees aching, I decide I better head home. When I turn onto our block, I'm shocked and relieved to find Mama sitting on Miss Ada's stoop. Her suede pumps dangle from her hands and her blouse has come untucked from her skirt. The porch light comes on, revealing the tints in Mama's locks. Her makeup probably looked nice when she left the house, now Mama's eyes are ringed with dark smudges. I can tell she's been crying.

"You okay, Mama?" I ask as I let myself into the yard.

Miss Ada comes out onto the porch with a plastic shopping bag. She holds it out to me and places her palm on the top of Mama's head.

"She's fine, baby. My Eddie saw her at the station this morning and she was sitting on that same bench when he got back, so he brought her to me. You take your mama on home now, and fix her a little supper with what's in the bag."

I go up the steps to take the bag from her outstretched hand. "Thank you, Miss Ada."

"You don't got to thank me, child. We in this together. Don't you forget that."

I help Mama slide her feet into her shoes and hold her hand as she follows me down the steps and out to the street. When we get home, I go straight to the bathroom to wash my hands. Mama goes straight to her room and crawls into bed.

I use Mama's tweezers to pull the splinters out. Then I rub some stinging hand sanitizer on my palms and put a bandage over the cut. I creep into Mama's room, pick up all her clothes, and hang them in the closet. Mama wants her old life back, I know she does. But she's just not ready yet.

In Miss Ada's bag are two cans of Spam, a box of Rice-A-Roni, and a couple of small tomatoes from her garden. I find a can of peas and carrots in the cupboard and make a pretty decent stir-fry. I cover a plate with foil and leave it on the table for Mama. It's still there when I get up in the morning, so I put the plate in the microwave and have leftovers for breakfast.

It's Friday. When school ends, I will pick up Freddie and head to the cemetery. I will tell Cin that I accept her offer. I am going to find that door. I have to find us a way out.

7.

Today I don't waste time hanging around Clark Park. It's not exactly raining but the sky is gray and before long, mist wets my face and dampens my clothes. Freddie doesn't seem to mind the weather and he doesn't complain when we skip the tennis ball and head straight for The Woodlands.

At lunch I made a list of questions to ask Cin. The folded sheet of paper is wilting in my palm by the time I reach Section K. I find Cin standing under a tree, her eyes glued to the ground. Drew isn't around, which suits me since some of my questions are about him.

I draw closer but Cin doesn't look up or acknowledge me. I peer at the large bronze marker set in the ground. It reads,

HERE REST THE REMAINS
OF 437 PERSONS
REMOVED FROM A
FORMER BURIAL GROUND
OF THE CITY OF PHILADELPHIA'S
BLOCKLEY ALMSHOUSE,
1835 TO 1888,
DISCOVERED IN 2001
DURING EXCAVATION

FOR CONSTRUCTION AT
THE SOUTHEAST CORNER
OF UNIVERSITY AVENUE
AND CIVIC CENTER BOULEVARD

"Are you—I mean, were you buried here?"

Cin still doesn't look at me but she does shakes her head. "I never received a proper burial."

"Why not?"

She sighs and turns away from the marker. "Buzzards."

"Buzzards?"

"They preyed upon the poor and the Negroes. Dug up the bodies and sold them to the highest bidder."

"Who would pay for a dead body?" I ask, horrified.

"Medical students, doctors specializing in particular afflictions. We were not people to them, just tissue and organs and bones to be dissected and then discarded like offal in a slaughterhouse. The Resurrectionists, as they were called, became so bold that the Guardians built a vault to preserve the dead. But it made no difference. There were vultures within, too. No one could protect us."

I take a deep breath to stop my head from spinning. I'm almost afraid to ask but there's something I need to know.

"I've thought about your offer," I tell Cin. "You're right—I need to take my mother away from here. What did you mean when you said parts of you are missing? I mean, you look...whole."

"This is the form I choose."

I think about that for a moment. It feels like a riddle. "So...you could look different if you wanted to? Older—or younger? Or could you be a whole other species—like an animal?"

Cin glances down at Freddie before repeating, "This is the form I choose."

I don't want to unfold the damp square of paper in my hand, so I try to remember the questions I wrote down earlier.

"With Drew—does he really need that crutch? Couldn't he— shouldn't he be able to..." I sigh, frustrated by my inability to be direct. "Drew doesn't still need it to walk, does he?"

Nana always told me that in heaven the lame could walk and the blind could see. Any imperfection you had during life was fixed once you passed through the pearly gates. I don't tell Cin all of that but she must know what I'm thinking because she says, "Heaven is a fiction. So many stories are told to bind us to this world."

"If there's a door close by, could Drew leave, too?"

Cin nods. "He could, but that is not his choice."

"He'd rather stay here with you?"

"He takes some comfort in my presence but Andrew's loyalty belongs to another. There was a nurse who worked at Blockley. Mrs. Acton was her name. Andrew was a favorite of hers."

I think back to the way Drew shrieked with delight each time Freddie hurried back to him with the stick clamped between his teeth. "I can see why. He's a sweet kid."

Cin frowns. "Andrew's merits are evident to us. But you have to understand that to many, the inmates at Blockley were repulsive. We were to be pitied and tolerated and experimented upon—but not loved. How they thought they could ever heal bodies they despised, I do not know. After the collapse, when the rubble had been cleared, Mrs. Acton wept over Andrew's mangled body. He had rarely known such devotion in his short life. Genuine love is a rarity in any world. Andrew was blessed to find it here and so here he remains."

"What collapse?"

For the first time, Cin looks surprised. Perhaps she didn't mean to tell me about that. I have other questions on my list but before I can ask one she says, "Walk with me."

We pass the community garden, the carriage house, and the beehives. Cin says nothing but once we reach the worn dirt path, her words start to flow.

"When the ship reached the Sea Islands, I was sold. There was a woman, Mem, who took care of me. I was weak and feverish, but she nursed me back to health. Mem was a healer and a midwife. She traveled all over the county catching babies in the quarters and the big house. Mem was losing her sight. She taught me everything she knew and before she passed, she brought my own child into this world."

"You have kids?"

"One. Having such a valuable skill made my life a bit easier than most slaves. In time, I told Mem about my gift and as we went from plantation to plantation, she told the seekers when an open door was nearby."

"Seekers—you mean runaways?"

Cin nods at me. "We did what we could for those who were willing. Then Mem died. Not long after I was sold with my daughter, and then bequeathed to my last mistress. She was just a child at the time and living in Delaware. When she left for finishing school in Boston, she took my daughter as her maid.

"In Boston she met a Quaker girl from Philadelphia. She was an ardent abolitionist. They fell in love and my mistress had a change of heart. First she freed my daughter and then she freed me. We made a home together in Philadelphia. For a time, we were happy."

If Cin finds pleasure in that memory, her face shows no sign. I walk beside her, respectfully silent. Cin is just a few inches from me but I feel her drifting away. I finally break the silence in order to bring her back.

"You said some people thought of you as a murderer. Why?"

"I told you that my mistress asked for my assistance."

"She needed a way out?"

"She did, and so I showed her where to find a door. Her lover agreed to meet her there. My mistress packed her most precious possessions and bid us farewell. But when the time came, her lover's courage failed. When my mistress realized she had been forsaken, she let the door close, filled her pockets with stones, and threw herself into the river."

I shiver and look past the trees to where the Schuylkill still flows. Cin's story sounds like something from a fairy tale but I know she isn't making this up.

"When they found her bloated body, her family couldn't bear the shame of suicide. So they blamed me for her death. Her fickle lover denied all knowledge of the elopement and claimed I had lured my mistress across the river in order to rob her. I should have hanged but a young doctor arranged to have me brought to Blockley instead. My mistress had spurned him when he proposed years before. Back then he was just a poor medical student from South Carolina. He blamed me for his rejection."

"Did he know about your gift?"

"He accused me of witchcraft, devilry…he came to be revered in his field and yet the man held theories that were not compatible with a rational mind. But he had instruments at his disposal and complete authority over the inmates. He had wealth, status, the respect of his peers. No one questioned his methods or his motives."

"And this doctor—he's the one who stole your parts?"

Cin nods and her lips twist into a snarl as she shares the bitter memory. "He harvested them once I was dead. In life, he was my tormentor. When the asylum collapsed, I thought fate had finally placed me beyond his reach. But I was wrong."

She pauses and her hand drifts from her waist to clutch her belly. "My only comfort is that he never touched my daughter. She fled the city after I was sent to Blockley. In spite of his many violations, he could not break our line."

"What happened to your daughter?" I ask.

"Liza went north to Canada but returned after just one year. In the last letter I received from her, she said she was thinking of heading home—to Sierra Leone."

"You never saw her again?"

"No, but I could sense her spirit. She lived a long life, as did the children she birthed. The gift has been passed from mother to daughter. Our work continues."

Cin looks at me and seems to read my mind. "In your heaven, the dead are reunited with those they have lost. A comforting tale. The truth is that when we die, the doors to all worlds open wide."

A flash of red catches my eye and I look up to see a pair of cardinals disappear into a holly bush. The muted coloring of the female bird makes it easy for her to hide, but I still glimpse her between the dark, spiky leaves.

"So...can you find Liza again? Or will your daughter be able to find you?"

"Yes—once I am whole."

I glance at the sodden square of paper in my hand. So many of the questions I wanted to ask now seem pointless. Cin seems to be done talking because she turns and heads back up the path.

I trail after her, wanting our conversation to continue. I clear my throat and say, "You were going to tell me about the collapse."

Cin slows for just a moment before gliding on at her usual brisk pace. The path splits in two and I speed up so I can walk beside instead of behind her.

"The Guardians were appointed to oversee the operation of the almshouse. But money meant for our care was sometimes squandered, goods were stolen, corners were cut whenever possible. Infants in particular suffered terribly. Dozens upon dozens died every year.

"At last the Guardians resolved to heat the building properly. But the work was shoddy and over time, the structure became unsound. Early one morning in 1864 the women's ward of the asylum simply collapsed without warning, burying us alive. Over a dozen of us perished and many more were injured."

Buried alive! I try to imagine what I would do if my school suddenly collapsed around me. Then I look at Cin, at the way she walks with confidence and dignity despite all the terrible things that have been done to her. I can't turn back time, but maybe I can do something now to make things right. I want a chance to start over with my mother. Cin deserves a chance to do the same with her daughter.

"I'm sorry that happened to you—all of it. And I want to help you, I really do. But how will I find the parts that were taken from you? A lot of time has passed and I don't even know where to look."

I want to add, "I'm just a kid," but who cares about that? I don't need Cin to feel sorry for me. A lot of stuff happened to her when she was just a kid. I take care of Mama the best I can, and I'm going to do my best for Cin, too.

"They are close—I can sense them," she says with a faraway look in her dark eyes. "They are waiting to be reclaimed."

That doesn't really help me but I nod just the same. "Do you know the name of the doctor who...operated on you?"

"McConnell. Dr. Gerald McConnell."

Cin spits his name out. I hear the contempt in her voice and wonder if this famous doctor is buried here in The Woodlands. I would never desecrate a grave but people sometimes protest to have statues taken down. Just because he was respected back in the day doesn't mean I have to respect him now. People should know what he did to Cin. Too bad I won't be around to tell that story. I'll find Cin's missing pieces and then I'll take Mama to another world.

That reminds me of my most important question. "Tell me again how to find the door. The city's full of them. You said it's close by?"

Cin nods. "When I was alive, I could always sense the presence of a door. It would appear as a candle's flicker, a blink of the sun.

Each door is like a seam about to burst. I could always feel the tension. But now…you will have to use your senses. Mine have been impaired."

I frown. "I'm looking for a flicker?"

I must sound as hopeless as I feel because Cin stops walking and turns to face me.

"Do not despair. The door will bear my mark. You need not pass through it right away. Once opened, it will remain that way for three days and three nights. Then the door will close."

Cin moves past me and abandons the path to weave through the graves. I turn to follow her but trip over a braid of exposed tree roots and find myself sprawled on the muddy ground. By the time I get up, Cin is gone.

8.

My hand won't stop throbbing. I put another bandage on it but it won't stop bleeding, either. And it still hurts—a lot. I lie awake thinking about what that lady on the street said. Do I need a tetanus shot? I can't get sick, not now. I have to find the door! Then I'll figure out how I'm going to convince Mama to leave everything behind. Not everything—she'll still have me. We'll have each other. That's enough.

It's after midnight when I get out of bed and pull my hoodie over my pajamas. The TV's on in Mama's room so she doesn't hear me creep down the stairs and out of the house. I retrace my route from the night before until I find the house on the corner where I lost my breath. The streets are mostly empty at this time of night but I'm still grateful for the cover the fog provides.

Relief helps to steady my nerves. I didn't dream it—the white door is still propped against the side of the wrecked building. It glows softly in the dark, strangely perfect despite the chaos surrounding it. I glance around to see if anyone's watching, and then climb the shifting mound of rubble to reach the house. With my heart thudding in my ears, I grab hold of the glass doorknob and pull. The door must be solid wood because I have to use both hands to lift it away from the wall of the house.

Before I can see the other side, I get sucker punched again. Actually, this time it feels as if a hand has reached into my chest and wrapped itself around my lungs. I struggle to breathe but manage not to fall down this time. I cling to the door, determined to see what's on the other side. With my feet sliding back down the mound of debris, I finally manage to flip the door over. The back, like the front, is freshly painted. But on this side, near the knob, is a bloody hand print.

The fog thickens, making it hard to see. My chest tightens, making it hard to breathe. But in the jungle of a yard behind the ruined house I see a quick glimmer of light. A *flicker*.

I've found it.

This is the door!

And that gory red smear is Cin's mark.

When I get home, Mama is snoring softly in front of the TV. I turn it off and pull the covers up around her chin.

Mama's eyes flutter open. She lifts her hand and reaches out to touch my cheek. "Don't break my heart, baby," she whispers.

I wrap my fingers around hers and force myself to smile. "I won't, Mama. I promise."

Mama drifts off and I go to my room feeling weary but proud. I found the door! All I have to do now is hold up my end of the bargain. I start to make a plan to find Cin's parts but my eyelids are too heavy. I surrender and sleep soundly until a persistent fist starts pounding on our front door. Still groggy, I just manage to lift my head off the pillow when Mama calls out, "You have a visitor, Taj."

Before I can throw back the covers and swing my legs over the edge of the bed, Janae saunters into my room.

Anger flares inside of me, making me instantly alert. "What are *you* doing here?"

"We have a project to work on for school, remember?" Janae

says loudly enough for Mama to hear. Then she closes the door behind her and gets in my face. "Where'd you go last night?"

"What? Mind your business, Janae," I hiss.

"Juan told my aunt he saw you out on your own after midnight. I know exactly what a hustler like Juan's up to at that time of night. What were *you* doing, Taj?"

There's a knock at the door and Mama pops her head in. "You two want some breakfast? I could make pancakes."

Janae beams at Mama. "Thanks, Ms. Evie. I love pancakes…"

"We gotta go to the library, Mama. We don't have time to eat."

Mama nods but gives me a funny look before leaving us on our own.

I jump out of bed and throw open my bedroom door. "Get out!"

"I thought we were going to the library," Janae says, planting herself on the edge of my bed.

"I have to get dressed, don't I?" It's not a question I expect Janae to answer but she doesn't take the hint and leave.

"I've got two brothers, Taj. You ain't got nothing I haven't seen a hundred times before."

Last night I felt like I finally had everything under control. But right now Janae's got me feeling like I'm about to lose it. "GET OUT!" I yell.

"Is everything okay?" Mama calls from the living room.

Janae gets up and says in her sweetest voice, "Everything's fine, Ms. Evie. I guess Taj just needs a little privacy."

"Come keep me company, Janae. It's been ages since I've seen you. I can't believe how grown you look…"

I close the door to my room so I don't have to hear Janae sucking up to my mother. Mama seems to be in a good mood but that won't last if nosy Janae starts asking all kinds of questions. I throw on the same clothes I wore yesterday and grab my book bag. My breath isn't fresh but I'm not doing Janae any favors this morning.

"I'm ready. Let's go," I say as I head for the front door.

Mama and Janae are standing at the kitchen counter, spooning clotted cream and jam onto Mrs. Whitmore's scones. The kettle is about to shriek so Mama must be boiling water for tea. That was supposed to be for me—not Janae.

Mama frowns at me. "Wow, Taj. You sure know how to make a guest feel welcome."

She wasn't invited. That's what I want to say. But what comes out of my mouth is, "Janae can come by anytime. She knows that." I say it with as much sincerity as I can manage under the circumstances. And it's true—there's no stopping Janae.

She crams half a scone into her mouth and follows me to the door. Mama hurries over to give both of us a kiss on the cheek before sending us on our way.

When I reach the sidewalk and know Mama can't hear me, I say what's really on my mind. "You got a lot of nerve showing up at my house like that."

I'm not interested in what Janae has to say so I turn and head down the block without waiting for her response.

She calls after me, "Hey, Einstein—the library's this way."

I don't even bother to look over my shoulder. I need to talk to Marshall and he hangs out in the schoolyard sometimes. The tennis courts are another option and they're right across the street from our school. That's where I'm going.

"Oh, I get it," Janae says, hurrying to catch up with me. "You just lied to your mother so you could get rid of me. Well, I'm not one of your special ghost friends from the cemetery—I'm not going to just disappear."

I ignore Janae and keep walking at a pace that's hard for her to match. But she doesn't give up that easily.

"Why were you in the street last night, Taj?"

"I was looking for something," I mutter.

"At 1am?"

When I don't respond, Janae grabs my arm to slow me down. "Did you find what you were looking for?"

I jerk my arm away and say, "Yeah, Janae, I did. Happy? Why are you all in my business right now? I don't have time for this."

"Something's happening to you, Taj. Ever since you told us about that woman in the cemetery you've just been acting weird. Weirder than usual," she adds sarcastically.

I'm so angry right now that I can hardly speak. I feel like my throat's closing but fury forces words to fly from my mouth. "This isn't about me. And it's not about you! Everything isn't *for you*, Janae! It's for *her*..."

My voice cracks, betraying me. Hot tears erupt unexpectedly and spill like lava down my cheeks. "Just leave me alone," I whisper, turning away to hide my shame.

Janae says nothing for a moment but I can tell she's still standing behind me. When I dare to glance at her over my shoulder, she takes a step closer and clears her throat. "Who's it for?" she asks softly.

"What?"

"This thing you went looking for in the 'hood in the middle of the night. You said it's not for you. So who's it for, Taj?"

I sigh and feel the rage draining out of me. "It's for my mother, okay? It's...the closest I can get to a cure. I'm going to take her away from here—to a place where she can get better."

"Where is this place, Taj?"

I lower my eyes and say nothing. Janae senses my uncertainty and spins me around to face her.

"Oh my God, Taj. Please tell me you aren't going to join that graveyard lady's cult!"

I shake my head and more tears spill from my eyes. "This is something I have to do on my own, Janae. Just leave me alone."

"Where are you going—really?"

"To find Marshall," I say, heading up the block.

Janae follows me. "I thought you had to do this on your own."

She actually sounds hurt—maybe even a little jealous. But I don't have time to worry about Janae's feelings right now.

"Marshall doesn't hassle me," I tell her. "And he doesn't spy on me, either. He trusts me to make the right choice."

"They."

"What?"

"Marshall doesn't use 'he' and neither should you when you're talking about them. Use 'they.' *They* don't hassle you like I do."

We're almost at the schoolyard. I stop walking and try one last time to get rid of Janae.

"You want to know what I was looking for last night?"

Surprised, Janae jams her hands in her pockets and nods once.

I take a deep breath and hope the truth will scare her off. "I found a portal, Janae. A door to another world. A door the ghost lady in the cemetery told me how to find."

Janae pulls her hands out of her pockets and folds her arms across her chest. Right now she looks just like Aunt Jackie, but I'm not afraid. I brace myself for what Janae will say next.

"Another world, huh?"

I nod.

"Tell me about it."

"What?"

"You're taking your mother to a better place. What's it like?"

I glance down the block to the schoolyard. I can hear skateboards flipping and crashing on the asphalt.

Janae reads me like a book.

"You don't even know, do you? Oh my God. You're taking your poor mother to this place when you don't even know if it's *safe*? Who do you think you are, Taj—Christopher Columbus? That jerk *ruined* the so-called 'New World.' And it wasn't empty when he got there—

look what he did to the Native Americans! What if *you* carry a disease to this other world?"

"It won't be like that," I insist but even I hear the doubt in my voice. "We just need a way to start over..."

"And what makes you so special, Taj? How come your family deserves a way out but not the rest of us?"

"Wait a minute—you just said I don't know where I'm going. Now you're saying *you* want to go, too?"

Janae sighs but I can't tell if she's frustrated with me or with herself. "That's not what I'm saying. You can't just give up, Taj. I know things have been hard for you and your mom..."

"No—you *don't* know what it's like. You don't see her when she's curled up under the covers and I can't get her to eat or take a shower or even get dressed. She's *my* mother—*my* responsibility. I'm all she's got left."

"And what about the rest of us? Why do you get to check out when the rest of us have to keep on struggling? You don't think I wish I could have helped *my* mother?"

I didn't see that coming. "You never even talk about her," I say awkwardly.

Janae starts blinking real fast and I realize the shine in her eyes isn't from anger—it's tears. I've never seen her like this before.

"Talk about her? What is there to say? She's gone. GONE, Taj! Out there chasing her next high...the mother I knew is never coming back. Sometimes you just have to let folks go."

I shake my head. "I hear what you're saying, Janae, really I do. But I've let go of too many folks already. I'm not letting go of Mama. She's coming with me."

"Have you asked her? Have you told her about this...weird door?"

I look away from Janae's piercing black eyes. "Mama can't think straight right now."

"Neither can you, apparently."

For a moment we just glare at each other.

"Think about it, Taj. Let's assume this door is real—"

"It *is* real," I insist. "I've seen it."

Janae holds up her hands in mock surrender. "Fine. There really is a door in West Philly that will take you to another world. Where would we be if everyone just gave up and split when times got tough?"

"But we *have* been doing that. Some of us, at least. Folks on slave ships jumped overboard, runaways followed the North Star to freedom. And look at Marcus Garvey—he knew we didn't truly belong here. Paul Robeson went to Russia. Marshall told me James Baldwin lived in France for a while."

"So did Josephine Baker. Lots of African American artists went overseas back in the day. What's your point?"

"My point is, Black people have been getting beat down for hundreds of years—slavery, segregation, and now we got these trigger-happy cops out here. You really think all of us should just stick around and take it?"

"I didn't say that. Black people have come a long way and that's because a whole lot of us fought back, Taj. Our ancestors didn't take it and they didn't run away. They thought about future generations and not just themselves. You think Mr. Jackson would want you to disappear through some door?"

That's a low blow. I can't look Janae in the eye, which gives her the confidence to press on.

"If Mr. Jackson were here today, he'd tell you to man up! You know I'm right. You don't just belong to yourself or your mother. You belong to us! People make up families, and families make up neighborhoods, and together we make a community. Believe it or not, we need you, too, Taj."

I want to say something about how before this week, Janae

hardly ever talked to me. I want to remind her that she changed into a hyena last year and only just started taking an interest in my life. Instead I say, "You should meet Cin. It makes more sense when she breaks it down."

Janae's eyes open wide. "*Sin*? You're getting advice from some woman named SIN?"

"It's short for Lucinda. And she's seen it all, Janae—the slave ships, the plantations. They thought she was crazy so they locked her up in this asylum. But they weren't really treating the patients—they were experimenting on them. And then the almshouse collapsed and now she's a ghost. But she still knows where all the doors are."

I stop talking and take a good look at Janae. She's sucked in her lips and is just staring at me, hard. I can tell what she's thinking and figure I might as well say the words out loud.

"It's true. Call me crazy if you want—that's just a word people use to dismiss folks who see the world differently. I don't care how it sounds. It's true—all of it. Cin wants to help me."

"What if your mother doesn't want that kind of help?"

She's got me there. I try to think of something to say, but that's the question that's been keeping me up at night. *What if Mama won't go?*

"Hey, y'all. What's up?"

We look across the street and see our classmate Ronell. He doesn't really go to school anymore but I still see him on the street sometimes. Last I heard he was working for Juan. I don't know if that's true, but Ronell definitely didn't get those fly kicks and that gold chain walking dogs and cutting grass.

I lift my chin at Ronell and he nods backs. Janae waves, which earns her a nervous smile from the lanky boy.

With her eyes still on Ronell Janae says, "He thinks we're talking about him."

"We *are* talking about him," I point out.

Janae turns back to me. "Not really. I'm just going to use Ronell to make my point."

"Which is?" I ask impatiently.

"Ronell is Ronell. Right? If you picked him up and dropped him anywhere else in the world, he'd still be Ronell. He'd still make the same bad choices. You think going someplace different is going to solve your problems, but you'll still be you. Your mother...what's going on inside of her mind..."

My cheeks burn but I hold her gaze. It's Janae who loses her nerve and looks away first. I don't know why that makes me feel powerful but I stand a little taller. Janae takes a step back and sighs before looking me in the eye again.

"Changing what's on the outside won't necessarily fix what's on the inside, Taj. That's all I'm trying to say."

Janae shrugs and I take that to mean she's finally run out of words. I give her a tiny nod and say, "I hear you. But I gotta do what I gotta do."

"Whatever, Taj. Have fun tumbling down that rabbit hole."

On any other day, I'd probably be happy to know that Janae still cares about me. And if she had said she wanted to come with us, I'd probably let her tag along. But today I have more important things to worry about. So I watch as Janae heads back to our block, and then I walk over to the schoolyard hoping I'll find Marshall there.

9.

I spot Marshall and wave as I cross the schoolyard. A bunch of little kids are playing on the monkey bars and three guys are shooting hoops on the concrete court. One of them is Mike Avery.

Marshall glides over to meet me. He hops off the skateboard and flips it upright with his foot. *Their*—not his. Their foot.

I open my mouth but no words come out. I wonder when Marshall switched from "he" to "they." I feel bad that Janae knew about it and I didn't. I think about all the times I must have offended Marshall by using the wrong pronoun.

"You okay?" Marshall asks.

"Yeah. I—I just need your help."

Marshall glances over at the basketball court. "With what?"

"Uh...a research project."

"Your biography of Paul Robeson?"

I shake my head and try to block out all the doubts Janae has planted in my mind. Then I take a deep breath and ask, "Your folks work at Penn, right?"

Marshall tilts his—*their* head to one side the way Freddie does sometimes. It almost makes me laugh but I can't afford to be silly right now.

"My dad does. He teaches in the School of Ed," Marshall tells me. "But Mom works at Drexel. She's an archivist."

I let out a sigh of relief. "Would your mom know anything about medical specimens?"

Marshall studies me for a moment. "What's going on, Taj? Janae's been texting me. She's worried about you."

I try to smile but my mouth won't cooperate so I just shrug instead. "You told me to trust my gut. Remember?"

Marshall nods. "What's it telling you to do?"

I don't have time to make up a story so I tell Marshall the truth. "I made a deal with the ghost woman in the cemetery. I have to help her if I want her to help me."

"Sounds fair. What kind of help does she need?"

This is where is gets weird. But Marshall's the most open-minded person I know, so I give it to them straight. "She needs me to find some body parts. After she died she was…dissected. Without her permission. Now she wants her parts back."

Marshall says nothing for a long time. Then they pull out their phone and start texting someone. "My mom doesn't work at the medical college," Marshall explains, "but she can access records from all over the city."

A few seconds later, Marshall's phone pings and I lean in to see what Mrs. Sanders has texted back.

"She says it's almost impossible to trace cadavers used for medical research in the nineteenth century—especially the ones used without consent."

I don't even try to hide my disappointment. Then the phone pings again and my heart leaps. I wait anxiously for Marshall to share the second text.

"Hm. Mom says if you have the name of a particular doctor, you might be able to trace a collection of specimens. They were sometimes donated to medical schools or museums."

"I know his name! It's Dr. McConnell."

"First name?" Marshall asks.

"Gerald."

I watch as Marshall texts the name to their mother. The phone pings again and Marshall scans the screen before putting the phone back in their pocket. "She'll do a quick search and see what comes up."

"Thanks, Marshall. I really appreciate your help—and your mom's."

Marshall shrugs like it's no big deal. "Mom lives for stuff like this. She's like a librarian on steroids! The more obscure the subject, the better. If she finds anything, I'll let you know."

I grip the straps of my book bag. There's not much in it right now but I still feel tired, like I've been carrying a heavy load too far for too long.

Marshall glances over at the court again. The game is wrapping up and this time Mike gives Marshall a nod.

"Are you guys—I mean, are you two going to hang out later?" I ask.

Marshall nods but quickly changes the subject. "So this deal you made with the ghost—once you find her parts, what will she do in return?"

"There's a portal in my neighborhood. Cin's going to tell me when it's open. I'm going to take my mom away from here." When Marshall's eyes open wide I hurry to add, "It's the only way she'll ever get better."

Marshall's phone pings again. They pull it out and scan the screen.

"Huh. Mom says a Dr. Gerald McConnell donated his collection of medical curiosities to that wacky museum we went to last year. Remember?"

I do. At the time it seemed like the best field trip ever. I was right there with the rest of my classmates, laughing and pointing at the glass cases holding unborn babies in jars, dried up hands and feet, wax molds of faces disfigured by disease, and the skeleton of a dwarf next to one of a giant. Back then I didn't think about where all those skulls and organs and bones came from. They belonged to freaks, not people like me. People like Cin.

Suddenly my blood starts to boil like lava under my skin. I feel ashamed and wish I had thought to ask someone at the museum where all those body parts came from. Why did our teacher even take us there?

"You okay?" Marshall asks.

It's getting hard to breathe but I clear my throat and say, "I'm fine. I just don't understand why Cin would be put on display. She's—"

I stop before the word "normal" comes out of my mouth. McConnell probably wanted to find the source of her "gift." Or maybe he just wanted to make Cin pay for what happened to the woman he loved. Either way, cutting her up is the ultimate disrespect. He had no right to take anything from Cin—alive or dead.

I look up and realize that Marshall's still watching me. "Cin's special," I say quietly.

"So were all the people who wound up in that museum. Something about their bodies or their brains made them different, and that made them 'interesting' to science. Museums never put their entire collection on display so they've probably got more specimens in storage. Your ghost's missing organs could be in the basement."

My mouth is dry as a desert but I can feel my eyes filling up with tears. "I have to go," I say abruptly.

Marshall lets the skateboard drop and gets ready to push off. "If you need any more help, just let me know. I'm sure Janae would help, too."

I groan and Marshall says, "I know she can be kind of prickly sometimes, but Janae cares about you, Taj."

I kick at a glob of gum on the concrete and blink away my tears. "She thinks I'm giving up. She thinks I'm a coward."

"That's not true. Janae's lost some important people in her life," Marshall reminds me. "She probably just doesn't want to lose you, too."

I turn to go and then remember one more thing I need to ask Marshall. "Are you busy after school on Monday?"

"Why?"

"Can you meet me at the cemetery? I'm going to need you to take Freddie home."

"No problem, Taj."

"In fact, Mrs. Whitmore is going to need a new dog walker. The job's yours if you want it."

Marshall nods and checks the court once more.

"Just one last thing, Marshall."

"Yeah?"

"On Monday—come alone."

Marshall nods and pushes off. I watch as the skateboard carries them across the court to where Mike is waiting.

10.

Now that I'm leaving, I notice everything in my neighborhood. As I walk to The Woodlands for the last time, I take a picture in my mind of all the people and places I'm going to miss. But I keep on walking. I leave them behind like the brightly colored berries that the birds won't eat.

I've only known Drew for a week but saying goodbye to him just about breaks my heart. When I reach the cemetery on Monday to take Freddie on his last walk (with me, anyway), Drew is waiting for me. Not in Section K where I normally meet him. This time Drew is waiting for me just inside the gate.

"You're leaving soon," he says with a strange smile.

My throat aches so I just nod and we start up the dirt path together. It hasn't rained yet today but the fine mist makes everything feel damp. I walk slowly to make the moment last and to make sure that Drew doesn't get tired. If he were alive today, maybe doctors could do something for him—put braces on his legs or give him exercises to strengthen his muscles. Then I think about what Cin said, how Drew's disability is part of who he is. I'm glad I got to know him in the form he chose.

"I've found someone else to walk Freddie," I tell him.

Drew tries to smile but he looks as miserable as I feel. "They won't see me. No one else ever does. Only you."

The ache in my throat sharpens and before I know it, I start to bawl. I drop to the ground and bury my face in the wet grass.

Drew hovers over me, his small voice soft in my ear.

"Don't cry, Taj. I'll miss you but I'm glad you've chosen to use the door. And you're helping Cin, too. I think you're really brave."

I clutch at the grass until my tears stop falling. Then I sit up and take a few deep, shaky breaths. It's a while before I can speak again but Drew patiently waits beside me. Freddie licks my hand and tries to get me to rub his belly.

"You're shameless," I tell him before giving in.

Drew grins and watches as I stroke the little dog. My eyes fill up with tears again but I manage to say, "I'm really glad I met you, Drew. And I want to thank you for introducing me to Cin. You changed my life…"

My voice gives out and I use my sleeve to wipe my eyes. "I won't forget you," I promise.

"I'll remember you, too, Taj. It's time to for me to go."

Drew turns and I follow his gaze over to where Cin is standing. She holds her hand out and Drew makes his way over to her. I can't hear what Cin is saying, but Drew listens closely to what seems like instructions. Then he turns and waves at me before disappearing into the mist.

I get up and walk over to where Cin is standing. "I found the door," I tell her.

Cin nods solemnly but says nothing so I go on.

"And I think I've found your parts. McConnell donated his collection of specimens to a museum in Center City. Can you—? I—I could take you there."

Cin nods once more and waits for me to lead the way. When I reach the cemetery gate, I see Marshall's waiting for me—and so is Janae. She's pacing back and forth on the sidewalk but when she sees me, she stops. Then her gaze goes past me and Janae's mouth falls open.

I glance over my shoulder. Nobody's behind me. Just Cin.

With their eyes only on me, Marshall comes up to take Freddie's leash. "Sorry, Taj. I tried to do like you said but...she insisted."

"It's okay," I tell Marshall. "Thanks for taking Freddie—and for everything else. You're a good friend, Marshall."

Marshall gives me a hug and says, "Good luck with everything." Then they head down Woodland Avenue with Freddie barking wildly at a pair of cyclists.

Janae is still staring past me so I finally ask, "Can you see her?"

Janae leans in and whispers, "Of course, I can see her—she's standing right behind you!"

"Marshall didn't see anything."

"I guess I'm special," Janae says with just a hint of sarcasm. "How are you going to get her to the museum?"

"What do you mean?"

Janae is clearly trying hard not to freak out. "What do I *mean*? She's a *ghost*, Taj! Can she, like, fly or something?"

"Stop hissing at me, Janae."

She presses her lips together and tries to calm down. "So what's your plan?"

I nod at the station across the street. "I figured we'd take the trolley."

Janae nods but she looks worried. "I hope you know what you're doing, Taj."

I take a deep breath and say, "I have to hold up my end of the deal."

Janae just looks at me. We pretty much said everything we had to say on Saturday, so I wait for Janae to walk away. Instead she steps past me and introduces herself to Cin!

"I'm Janae. Taj is my friend. Is it okay if I go with you to the museum?"

Cin looks at me but I can't think of anything to say. She turns back to Janae and nods.

"Great! Let's go," Janae says brightly.

You don't have to do this. I know that's what I ought to say but the truth is, I don't really want to make this trip on my own.

Janae links her arm through mine and together we form a kind of shield between Cin and the real world. Cin says nothing but stays close to us and together we manage to cross the busy avenue.

There are a few people waiting at the shelter but no one seems to notice Cin. Janae's trying not to stare but she can't keep her eyes off the somber ghost.

"I guess she pays the senior fare, huh?"

That's a decent joke but I'm too nervous to laugh right now. If Janae can see Cin, maybe other folks can, too.

"Let's get on at the back," I suggest as our trolley pulls up to the shelter. We let the passengers get off before climbing the stairs and moving to the last row.

Janae takes a seat and looks up at me expectantly. I turn to Cin. "Do you want to sit down?"

Cin shakes her head and keeps her gaze locked on the back window of the trolley. There aren't many passengers heading into the city at this time of day, and we go underground right away so there's not much to see besides the orange lights on the tunnel walls.

Janae watches Cin and pulls me down to whisper, "I think she's trying to keep her balance. When dancers have to spin around and around, they focus on one point and it keeps them from getting dizzy."

That makes sense. I can only imagine how Cin must feel. The last time she took a ride it was probably in a horse and buggy, and now she's in an electric trolley underground. We don't have far to go but the silence between us is agonizing. Janae's trying not to stare but she's failing miserably. Finally she gets up and whispers, "Is she okay?"

I'm not sure. Cin looks terrible. We left the cemetery just a few minutes ago yet in that time her skin has turned ashy and gray, and the neat bun at the back of her head has started to unravel. No one has touched her and Cin's not holding onto anything. She sways unsteadily as the trolley stops at each station before surging forward.

"We're almost there," I assure her. "Just a few more stops."

Her eyes don't meet mine but Cin nods to show that she understands. Finally it's our turn to get off the trolley. Cin is moving more slowly than before. It's like she's coming apart with each step. Her dress, plain but always tidy, is now dusty, rumpled, and torn at the shoulder. Dark stains appear near her waist and the sticky dark substance seems to be blood. Her head droops to her chest unless Cin props it up with her hand. The other she holds out before her as if feeling for a doorknob that is just out of reach.

The museum is in an old brick building wrapped in a tall fence made of cast-iron spikes. On one side is a garden and Cin drifts toward it, breathing heavily. She practically falls into the fence but then seems to grow calm as she breathes in the scent of plants flowering on the other side.

"Do you need something?" I ask, remembering Cin's knowledge of medicinal herbs.

"No time," she whispers, staggering back from the fence.

Together we slowly climb the steps that lead up to the museum's entrance. While Janae and I buy our tickets, Cin wanders over to a giant portrait of a White man that hangs in the lobby.

"Do you know him?" I ask, checking the name engraved on a golden plate at the bottom of the painting.

Cin drifts away without answering. We pass a marble staircase that leads to the second floor and enter the main gallery. A security guard greets us and reminds us that photography is not allowed. I fight to breathe normally and am grateful that Janae has linked her arm through mine once more.

If Cin is outraged, it doesn't show. She calmly glides past the glass cases, taking in all the objects on display. It's only when we reach the stairs leading to the lower level that I realize Cin isn't calm at all. Rage radiates like heat from her shattered body.

"Do you want to go downstairs? Maybe what you're looking for is—"

"I have seen enough," Cin says in a low voice that makes Janae clutch my hand.

"Leave me," she commands.

"What are you going to do?" I ask meekly. Part of me is terrified of what Cin could do, but another part of me wants to protect her. I can't leave her here alone.

Janae tugs at my hand. "We should go, Taj."

I know she's right but I'm not ready to leave Cin alone in this terrible place.

"Leave me," she repeats wearily.

"Not till I know what you're going to do," I insist.

Cin sways, then grasps at the air and somehow steadies herself. "It is time for you to let go, Taj. You do not belong here. Go and find your future. I am going to bury dead."

My mind races. *Bury the dead.* What does that mean?

"I am ready to proceed. Tell those who would live they must leave."

I turn to Janae. "How am I supposed to do that?"

Janae frantically looks around the gallery. Her eyes fall on a red box halfway up the wall. "There's the fire alarm."

I stare at Janae, horrified. How can this be happening? Her eyes are bright with fear.

"Do it," she says softly. "You have to do it—*now.*"

I swallow and try to think of something more to say. Cin is coming apart before our eyes.

"You got her here. Now you have to respect her wishes. Let go, Taj."

Janae tugs at my hand again but I still don't move. I can't take my eyes off Cin who seems ready to perform some kind of ritual. She spreads her arms and closes her eyes. The lights above us flicker on and off, and as Cin slowly raises her hands, a black sea rises from the angry earth. Within seconds the lower gallery is flooded—glass shatters, wood snaps, and the metal banister groans as inky waves swirl and swell and swallow everything in sight.

I hear a roar in my ears, a chorus of pained voices crying out in agony—or relief. I see the terror in Janae's eyes as she pleads with me to go. I feel her warm hand tugging at mine but I cannot move. The rising sea is seductive and holds the promise of peace. I feel myself falling forward, over the railing, into the bottomless sea...

Janae races past me and smashes the fire alarm with her fist. Then, with a strength that surprises me, she grabs me by the collar. Janae drags me out of the gallery and we tumble out of the museum with the other panicked visitors.

There is a brief moment of confusion and then the real chaos begins. The ground beneath us shudders and we barely have time to get across the street before a deafening boom slams us to the pavement. Plumes of dust swallow us like a tsunami. I fall to my knees and rub at my eyes. The darkness Cin conjured surrounds me still and I feel myself sinking, drowning, joining the dead.

It's Janae who pulls me back to the surface. I feel her arms wrapped tightly around me, and for a while she just rocks me back and forth right there on the sidewalk. Sirens blare around us but Janae holds me together and in time my tears stop, the dust settles, and I'm able to see once more.

Before us is a mound of rubble where the museum once stood.

"She did it," I whisper. "Cin buried the dead."

The tracks on Janae's dust-covered face prove I'm not the only one moved to tears. I lace my fingers between hers, hoping my touch provides at least some of the comfort she's given me.

"What happens now?" Janae asks quietly.

First responders are flooding the scene. They try to bring order to the chaos—directing traffic, searching for survivors, and caring for the injured. Soon they'll reach us but I don't need their help. I know just what I have to do now.

Janae is waiting for me to answer her question.

"Now we go home," I say simply.

"You're going to stay?" she asks hopefully. "In this world?"

I shake my head and take in the destruction all around us. People already have their phones out so they can film the chaotic scene.

"I can't stay, Janae. If I let this chance pass, I'll always wonder what the other world was like."

"Make it up—build the world you want *here*, Taj. I'll help you..."

My mouth feels dryer than the dust on our skin. I swallow hard and say, "You're a really good friend, Janae. I'm sorry I can't be the friend you need me to be."

A police officer beckons to those of us huddled together on the sidewalk. We stand up and see that the cars we sheltered behind have been totaled. The young woman beside me kisses the crucifix dangling from the chain around her neck. Some older folks are weeping softly. All of us seem to realize this situation could have ended differently.

Janae and I let ourselves be herded toward the end of the block. The gray sky opens once more and fat raindrops pelt us, washing off the dust. Janae looks at me like she's seeing me for the first time. She pulls her fingers from mine and says, "Bye, Taj."

I watch as an EMT in a fluorescent vest hands Janae a bottle of water before wrapping a plastic poncho around her shoulders. She's a survivor—Janae will be okay.

I find my bearings and head back to West Philly. It's time to tell Mama about my plan. It's time to walk through Cin's door.

DISCUSSION QUESTIONS

- Taj is taking a big risk by trading the world he knows for one he doesn't. If you were in his shoes, what would you do?

- What is your definition of freedom? Imagine you are Janae. Select one of the three women on her list and explain how that performer has contributed to the struggle for freedom.

- Look up the freedom fighters chosen by Marshall and Taj. Now make your own short list. Is there someone in your city or town who has contributed to the struggle for freedom, now or in the past?

- Learn more about these Black women and their role in medical research. What should be done to honor the known and unknown people used in medical experiments?

  Lucy, Betsey, and Anarcha
  Henrietta Lacks
  Sara "Saartjie" Baartman
  Eunice Rivers Laurie

- J. Marion Sims attended medical college in Philadelphia. A Manhattan statue of Sims, the "father of modern gynecology," was recently taken down after protests by Black women. Does Sims deserve to be honored for his contributions to the field of medicine?

- What does it mean to "decolonize" an institution? What should be done with human remains that were acquired unethically by scientists or museums?

- Learn more about the tragic life and death of Kalief Browder. How did his family respond to the unjust treatment of their loved one? How can we support people in our families and communities who are suicidal?

- Find a group advocating for bail reform in your community. Activists like Angela Davis believe in prison abolition. Does our society need prisons? How else could we promote justice and protect the public?

- Can words that were originally offensive be reclaimed and redefined? Look online for a newspaper account of the 1864 collapse at Blockley Almshouse. Compare the language used then and now to describe disabled people. Do you use ableist terms? Learn more at Disability in Kid Lit: http://disabilityinkidlit.com/2016/07/08/introduction-to-disability-terminology/

- Marshall uses singular "they/them/their" instead of "he/him/his." Why is it important to use the correct pronouns when speaking to non-binary people? Learn more about gender-neutral pronouns: https://www.teenvogue.com/story/they-them-questions-answered

- Imagine this novel has a sequel and write the first chapter. Where is Taj? Is his mother better? What's happening in the lives of Marshall, Janae, and Drew? Will the friends see each other again?

ACKNOWLEDGMENTS

This is a work of fiction—speculative fiction. The Woodlands is real and the Blockley Almshouse did have a partial collapse in 1864 that killed close to twenty people (mostly women housed in the "insane department"). I used real locations and historical events in West Philly to create a recognizable world where the dead simply won't stay silent.

I spend a lot of time thinking about the past. I wrote my first ghost stories in Brooklyn and this novel is, in some ways, a remix of *Ship of Souls*. A friend encouraged me to change the ending of that novel; though D was ready to journey to another realm, he got left behind. With this novel, I let my protagonist make his own choice and Taj's decision reflects my own struggle to find sanctuary in these turbulent times. I moved to Philadelphia in late August and this novel started to take shape shortly after I began running in the historic cemetery. Learning about West Philly's past made me feel more connected to, and invested in, my new home. I hoped to produce something that would resonate with the young people in my community.

Over the years I have tried to be more open about my own struggles with mental illness. My paternal grandmother's name was Zetta Elliott. According to my father, that Zetta was committed to an asylum in Antigua when he was just a child. Before he left the Caribbean for Canada in the 1950s, my father was told that his mother had died. I've tried to locate a record of her time at the asylum but none exists. We have no photograph of my grandmother. All I have is her name.

Earlier this year I wrote a poem about the way mental illness has affected the women in my family. I concluded the poem this way: "Women like us may be wounded, but we can also heal. Women like us are not disposable./Women like us must testify."

Of course, far too many women never get the chance to tell their stories—especially when race, gender, class, and disability intersect.

In order to develop a historical fantasy in The Woodlands, I needed to find a nineteenth-century link between the cemetery and African Americans. I came across an article about the 2001 discovery of intact burials and human remains from Blockley; once I confirmed that the almshouse had "colored" inmates, Cin's story began to unfold.

I am a solitary person and I am solely responsible for any errors this novel may contain. But Cin's story could not have emerged without the help of many generous people: Emma Max gave me a tour of The Woodlands that included a stop at the Blockley marker in Section K; my cousin Kameelah Rashad shared her expertise as a psychologist; my friend Ira Dworkin recommended that I visit the Mütter Museum; he advised against going alone, and Claire McGuire kindly offered to come with me to provide moral support. As we sat in the garden trying to process our impressions of the collection, I told Claire how Cin would obliterate all the specimens at the end of my novel. Claire then informed me that a building had collapsed not far from the Mütter Museum. "So if she does bring the building down," said Claire, "there's precedent for that."

After touring the museum I went upstairs and met with Beth Lander, librarian at the College of Physicians, who kindly provided a number of useful resources. I am grateful for the support I received from a number of archivists, including Claire and her partner Matthew Lyons. Mark Lloyd, Director of the University Archives and Records Center at the University of Pennsylvania and Kelsey Duinkerken, Special Collections and Digital Services Librarian at Jefferson, also responded immediately to my online request for assistance. When I learned that J. Marion Sims had studied at Jefferson Medical College, I felt the loose threads of my story tightening. I knew about Lucy, Betsey, and Anarcha and once taught my college students about Sara "Saartjie" Baartman. The narrative I crafted about Cin is fictional but it is rooted in fact. When it comes to Black women's bodies being violated and exploited for medical research, there's precedent for that, too.

I am grateful that my friend Gabrielle Civil gave me Louise Erdrich's 2016 novel *LaRose*. People of African descent and Indigenous people around the world share this struggle to reclaim the remains of our ancestors. I don't believe museums should be destroyed but they must be decolonized.

My aunt had Down Syndrome and I grew up in a family that taught me to respect people with disabilities. I never use the "r-word" but I was disappointed when I realized that I regularly use other ableist language. I am thankful for the disability terminology and other resources provided by Corinne Duyvis and Kayla Whaley at *DisabilityinKidLit.com*. I continue to make mistakes but I am grateful for those disability activists who help me to learn and do better.

I received valuable feedback from my beta readers Ebony Wortham and Brenda Bonhomme. Brenda is also my neighbor and she's one of several people at Garden Court Plaza who went out of their way to help me settle in. I am especially thankful for my fairy godmother at Post Brothers who found me a way out and a way in.

I'd like to thank my agent Jennifer Laughran for understanding that some of the stories I write are more urgent than others.

Lastly, I thank the people of West Philly for creating such a welcoming community. I planned to move to Philadelphia fifteen years ago but the timing just wasn't right. I still work in New York but each time I return to Philly, I breathe a sigh of relief. There are so many stories to uncover. I thank my ancestors for guiding me home.

~ Zetta Elliott
10/29/2018

ABOUT THE AUTHOR

Born in Canada, Zetta Elliott moved to the US in 1994 to pursue her PhD in American Studies at NYU. Her poetry has been published in several anthologies, and her plays have been staged in New York and Chicago. Her essays have appeared in *The Huffington Post*, *School Library Journal*, and *Publishers Weekly*. She is the author of thirty books for young readers, including the award-winning picture book *Bird*. Her urban fantasy novel, *Ship of Souls*, was named a *Booklist* Top Ten Sci-fi/Fantasy Title for Youth; her YA time-travel novel, *The Door at the Crossroads,* was a finalist in the Speculative Fiction category of the 2017 Cybils Awards. Her picture book *Melena's Jubilee*, won a 2017 Skipping Stone Award, and *Benny Doesn't Like to Be Hugged* is a first-grade fiction selection for the 2019 Scripps National Spelling Bee. Three books published under her own imprint, Rosetta Press, have been named Best Children's Books of the Year by the Bank Street Center for Children's Literature; Rosetta Press generates culturally relevant stories that center children who have been marginalized, misrepresented, and/or rendered invisible in traditional children's literature. *Dragons in a Bag*, a middle grade fantasy novel, was published by Random House in October 2018. *Say Her Name*, a young adult poetry collection, will be published by Hyperion in 2019. Elliott is an advocate for greater diversity and equity in publishing. She currently lives in West Philly.

Learn more at www.zettaelliott.com

BOOKS FOR TEENS

A Wish After Midnight
Mother of the Sea
Ship of Souls
The Deep
The Door at the Crossroads
The Return

CPSIA information can be obtained
at www.ICGtesting.com
Printed in the USA
FSHW020955210820
73177FS